Against the Clock

Samantha Alexander lives in Lincolnshire with a variety of animals including her thoroughbred horse, Bunny, and a pet goose called Bertie. Her schedule is almost as busy and exciting as her plots – she writes a number of columns for newspapers and magazines, is a teenage agony aunt for BBC Radio Leeds and in her spare time she regularly competes in dressage and showjumping.

Also by Samantha Alexander
and available from Macmillan

RIDERS

1 Will to Win
2 Team Spirit
3 Peak Performance
4 Rising Star
5 In the Frame
7 Perfect Timing *June 1997*

HOLLYWELL STABLES

1 Flying Start
2 The Gamble
3 Revenge
4 Fame
5 The Mission
6 Trapped
7 Running Wild
8 Secrets

RIDERS

6

Against the Clock

SAMANTHA ALEXANDER

MACMILLAN CHILDREN'S BOOKS

First published 1997 by
Macmillan Children's Books
a division of Macmillan Publishers Ltd
25 Eccleston Place, London SW1W 9NF
and Basingstoke

Associated companies throughout the world

ISBN 0 330 34538 9

1 3 5 7 9 8 6 4 2

A CIP catalogue record for this book is available from the British Library.

Phototypeset by Intype London Ltd
Printed by Mackays of Chatham plc, Chatham, Kent.

For my Editor, Gaby Morgan. For your encouragement and support, and for bearing with me when deadlines loom.

Samantha Alexander and Macmillan Children's Books would like to thank *Horse and Pony* magazine for helping us by running a competition to find our cover girl, Sally Johnson. Look out for more about the **Riders** and **Hollywell Stables** series in *Horse and Pony* magazine and find out more about Samantha by reading her agony column in every issue.

Macmillan Children's Books would also like to thank Chris White; and David Burrows and all at Sandridgebury Stables, especially Toby and his owner Sylvie.

And finally thanks to Angela Clarke from Ride-Away in Sutton-on-Forest, Yorkshire for providing the riding clothes, hats and boots featured on the covers.

CHARACTERS

Alexandra Johnson   Our heroine. 15 years old. Blonde, brown eyes. Ambitious, strong-willed and determined to become a top eventer. Owns Barney, a 14.2 hh dun with black points.

Ash Burgess   Our hero. 19 years old. Blond hair, blue eyes, flashy smile. Very promising young eventer. He runs the livery stables for his parents. His star horse is Donavon, a 16.2 hh chestnut.

Zoe Jackson   Alex's best friend. 15 years old. Sandy hair, freckles. Owns Lace, a 14.1 hh grey.

Camilla Davies   Typical Pony Club high-flyer. 15 years old. Owns The Hawk, a 14.2 hh bay.

Judy Richards   Ash's head groom. 18 years old.

Eric Burgess   Ash's uncle. Around 50 years old. His legs were paralysed in a riding accident. He has a basset hound called Daisy.

Look out for the definition-packed glossary of horsey terms at the back of the book.

CHAPTER ONE

"I'm going to win Burghley!" I got off the Pony Club coach feeling intoxicated with ambition.

My boyfriend Ash Burgess fell in alongside me, reeling from my latest revelation. "But you've only just mastered a Pony Club one-day event, never mind about a four-star international competition." His ash-blond hair flopped forward covering his eyes. "Honestly, Alex, talk about running before you can walk. You're only just fifteen."

"Not now, you idiot." I opened Barney's stable door, letting him bulldoze straight into me, trailing hay over my shoulder. "It's a five year plan."

Barney was a 14.2 Arab/Connemara cross with a dun coat and a human personality. He was a rising star and a local hero and with any luck we were going to go right to the top of the junior eventing scene.

The Sutton Vale Pony Club had just returned from the first day of Burghley. We had watched the dressage and were discussing Mary Thompson on Star Appeal and Pippa Nolan's new skewbald

Bits And Pieces. We'd walked the cross-country course following two gorgeous Australian riders who'd explained how they would tackle the trout hatcheries and the coffin. I'd made a bet that the water would ride better on two long strides than three short ones. Zoe, my best friend, had somehow managed to get a sweatshirt signed by all the British riders. I'd spent half an hour chatting to Andrew Nicolson, which had enraged Ash who was having to mind the seven and eight year-olds who were getting hysterical on excitement and junk food. We'd spent half an hour trying to extricate one of the latest Sutton Vale members from a portaloo which reminded me of the Doctor Who TARDIS. I was exhausted and aching but the thrill of an international event was still coursing through my veins.

Barney pushed at his feed bucket and stood on my foot. My face puckered up with pain. Ash took pity and wrapped his arms around me.

"I will win that trophy," I mumbled, burying my head in his chest and gently rubbing one foot against the other.

"Yes, darling. Whatever you say, dear."

Ash, who was nineteen and already a professional three-day eventer himself, knew exactly how tough, heartbreaking and torturously unpredictable the sport was. But if you didn't aim for the stars, how were you ever going to get anywhere?

I tipped back my face and his lovely soft mouth came down on mine for a knee-trembling kiss. Even now, Ash still had the ability to set my heart thumping and I couldn't imagine my life without him.

"Alex?" He eased me back slightly and pulled a quizzical face. "What on earth have you got in your trouser pocket?"

"Oh that." His eyes narrowed as I yanked out a clod of turf and held it up like the crown jewels. "I dug it up from the showjumping arena – I thought you might like it as a present."

"We've got to do something!" Zoe and Camilla ambled into the yard, casting a half-hearted glance at their horses, Lace and The Hawk. "The old fossil will go berserk if we don't make an effort."

Cam used to be a member of the Pony Club brat pack but since she'd stabled The Hawk at the Burgess yard we'd managed to develop her human side. She was blonde and her face was usually plastered in make-up, but at the moment she was trying to impress a guy called Aaron who wanted to be a deep-sea diver and favoured the natural look.

Zoe was trying to work out the difference between Irish and English martingales for a competition in a pony magazine as well as ripping off the wrapping from a Bounty bar and holding

3

on to a plastic manger she'd bought from one of the Burghley trade stands.

"Let's just take him to Alton Towers and be done with it." She plonked the manger down and smoothed out her sandy curls.

"Don't be stupid." Cam's eyes widened in disdain, taking her seriously. "He's in a wheelchair."

Eric Burgess was my trainer and mentor and now the main teacher at the Sutton Vale Pony Club. He had been crippled in a riding accident, and was probably the most cantankerous outspoken person you could ever wish to meet. But we all loved him to bits and he'd transformed us all from couch potatoes into serious competitors. It was his fiftieth birthday in a couple of weeks according to Ash, who was his nephew. We had to do something. And it had to be special.

"What about a meal out? Indian or Chinese," I proposed, bolting Barney's door and applying the special clip so he couldn't escape and do his usual trick of letting out all the other horses.

Ash, who was walking past with two brimming hay nets, nearly choked with shock. "Uncle Eric trying to roll up crispy Peking Duck pancakes? Give me a break." He bent down to switch on the outside tap and complained about a bad back. "The nearest Uncle Eric has come to a cultural experience is Yorkshire Pudding."

4

I lobbed a dandy brush at him for being so disrespectful and suggested the Sutton Vale Club call a meeting or at least arrange a kitty.

"Just keep old Brayfield out of the picture." Cam finally decided to feed The Hawk, who was on a new low-protein diet to knock some sense into him. "She'll have us passing the parcel and drinking orange squash."

Mrs Brayfield was the Pony Club secretary and well meaning, although a little highly strung. She'd probably benefit from high-fibre cubes more than The Hawk.

"I'll call a meeting," I announced, putting an end to the subject. "After all, we have got two weeks to organize it – how much time do we need?"

I decided to ride Barney in the manege for half an hour before I fed him, mainly because I was so fired up from Burghley I had to get in the saddle, feel the rhythm, the thrill.

Barney stomped out of the stable clearly annoyed, and sidled sideways every time I tried to get my foot in the stirrup. I gave him one of his favourite biscuits, rich tea covered with plain chocolate, and he spent so long sucking his gums that we were in the manege before he knew it.

Ash was busy getting Dolly ready for tomorrow. She was entered for the Burghley

Young Event Horse of the Future and considering she'd started off as a polo pony that wasn't bad going. She was a lovely flea-bitten grey 15.3 and as sharp as a greyhound. She was so talented that the main problem was not upgrading her too quickly. She'd won every novice event she'd been entered for and Ash thought she was a definite Olympic hopeful.

Barney thumped round the edge of the manege past the B marker refusing to stretch out his legs and humping his back like a camel. Barney loved to be the centre of attention and was clearly feeling neglected. Only yesterday my mother had been up for one of her weekly visits and Barney had run off with her handbag, bolting down the field with it clasped in his teeth.

I gave him fifteen minutes warming up and then started on some trotting poles and cavaletti, building up to small spreads. I'd typed out a list of Eric's tips and pinned them above my bed – now they were flitting in front of my eyes like the ten commandments.

If you look into the bottom of the fence, that's where you'll end up. Looking down unbalances the pony. Think where you're going next while the pony is in the air. Look beyond the jump when approaching. Don't drop the reins as you go over the fence. Fold forward from your hips and give with your hands as your pony pops over the fence . . .

I was so engrossed I didn't notice Ash stalking towards me, his face lit up like a Christmas tree. I didn't see his excitement. Not until he switched on the overhead lights and the arena flooded with light, blotting out the autumn evening shadows.

Ash clasped hold of Barney's reins, his eyes dancing with sheer adrenalin. "I've just had Sid Shackleton on the phone," he breathed and then paused for extra emphasis. "*The* Sid Shackleton."

I couldn't believe it. "Sid Shackleton, the dressage judge?" I was already trembling with anticipation.

Not only was he the leading dressage judge in the country, he was also in charge of the junior dressage team. He was like a god in the horse world.

"He wants to call in here now – on his way back from Burghley." Ash could hardly contain himself. "And it's not me he wants to see."

"Oh." My heart fluttered and flipped and I fiddled with Barney's reins. Then realization grabbed hold. "You mean me!" I was shell-shocked.

"Well, not exactly." Ash stroked Barney's custard-yellow coat as he stood chomping on his bit. But I wasn't listening. This could mean selection on a junior team.

"He was very specific . . ." Ash did his usual trick of breaking off mid-flow. It was as irritating as someone pressing the freeze button halfway through a film.

"He wants to see Barney."

CHAPTER TWO

"It can only mean one thing," I squawked, already frantic with the curry comb, "we've been discovered!"

Barney was munching his evening feed, unperturbed, spewing shreds of sugar beet all over the place and over-filling his mouth.

"You know I really think you ought to teach him some table manners." Camilla was spraying detangler into his tail and picking out the knots. Zoe was bent down slapping on hoof grease, which looked more like Fairy Liquid. We refused to use traditional hoof oil because it dried out the feet instead of conditioning them.

"It's not his table manners that Sid Shackleton's interested in," I barked. "It's his dressage!" I shook out the stable rubber and dipped it in the water bucket to wipe round Barney's head. "He must have spotted us at an event, you know, undercover. They have scouts out all the time, talent spotting."

Cam pulled a face and nearly zapped me with detangler. Zoe started larking around fitting an equine baseball cap to Barney's head collar which she'd bought at Burghley. It was the latest craze and there was a livery owner in the next stable with a Shetland pony called Arkle who had a different coloured cap for every day of the week. Horse owners were becoming like dog owners; any novelty idea became a craze. Next thing there would be an equine pooper shovel for taking with you out hacking.

"He's here!" Ash looked over the stable door, already changed into a clean shirt and distinctly whiffing of aftershave. "Alex, never mind Barney, brush your hair – you look as if you've been plugged into an electric socket."

The silver Range Rover glided into the yard exuding confidence and control if that was possible. Sid Shackleton filled the whole of the driver's side and had more jowls than a bloodhound. He had the air of someone who had been to hundreds of stable yards and was blasé about it all. There was a young girl sitting next to him with a cloud of dark hair, her face tight with anxiety. She must have only been seventeen.

Ash went across to the driver's door where Sid Shackleton had lowered the window. A few of the event horses poked their heads over their doors, naturally curious, dribbling hay everywhere but all looking very impressive. I wiped my hands behind my back on my jeans. Cam came up beside me wearing a huge floppy pink sweater with a

10

grass stain across her chest. The girl got out of the Range Rover and went straight across to Barney. He was licking the metal strip on the top of his door, which he always did after a feed. He had his eyes closed and no doubt was thinking about spring grass and good-looking mares.

Ash was still talking to Shackleton. I felt on edge and slightly at a loss as to what to do. The girl was staring at Barney as if in a trance. Even stranger, Barney had suddenly come to life and was going berserk trying to get closer to her.

A horrible cold feeling fluttered over me as if someone had walked over my grave. The girl was going into his stable.

"Hey!"

Sid Shackleton was out of the Range Rover and following her at a brisk march. He had the most enormous stomach which wobbled with every stride. Even Ash had difficulty keeping up with him.

Inside the stable the girl had her arms sprawled round Barney's neck, sobbing her heart out, her face pressed into his soft mane.

"Could somebody tell me what's going on?" My voice was quivering, an enormous wave of panic and jealousy rushing through me.

She looked up and stared straight at me, her mouth trembling with emotion, "I – I think Mr Shackleton had better explain."

*

11

Barney trotted up outside the stable, swinging his shoulders forward and striding out just like I'd taught him. I was out of breath after we'd gone just a few yards. My head was creaking, my heart was going through a minor earthquake. I couldn't believe what was happening. Ash, Camilla and the girl, who was called Claire, were all standing in a clump with Sid Shackleton, stony faced and awkward, not knowing how to act. Only Mr Shackleton was oblivious to the strain; he just watched Barney moving like a hawk, and allowed himself a small thin smile.

We pounded back towards them, Barney intent on getting in his stable to his hay net, his lovely tufty ears wafting back with irritation.

Ash was raking a hand through his hair, the other resting on his hip. He was tense with his teeth gritted and his mind whirring. He was desperately trying to get a grip of the situation. I could read it in his eyes. Panic.

"Well, Claire, are you a hundred per cent sure?" Mr Shackleton turned to the young girl whose eyes were still brimming with tears. Barney pushed his nose into her chest and then started sniffing her hair. He never did that to anybody but me. And only when I was upset. Claire reached out and tickled him under his chin. How did she know he liked that?

"That's him! That's my Dino!"

12

I was shaking with horror. It was impossible – Barney belonged to me.

"He's my horse, and I want him back." The girl tugged the lead rope out of my hand. "We'd better call the police right away!"

"Over my dead body!" I grabbed the lead rope back and clung on to Barney's head collar with both hands. "You're lying, you've got to be – my parents bought Barney fair and square."

Sid Shackleton stood there and insisted Barney had been stolen eighteen months ago from a field thirty miles away. Claire had been looking for him ever since.

"I don't believe you. You've got the wrong horse. You don't know what you're talking about."

I could hear the words coming out of my mouth but I was in numb shock. Later I couldn't remember a thing about what had happened – it was every horse owner's nightmare. But this wasn't something that had happened a few weeks ago, it was nearly two years. Surely even if the girl was telling the truth and Barney had at some stage been stolen, she wouldn't have a leg to stand on. I owned Barney. He was mine. For ever.

"I think you ought to leave." Ash stepped forward, rigid with fury. "How dare you come into my yard and make such wild accusations.

13

You're out of your tree. I know this pony very well and he hasn't been stolen, I can assure you."

"Don't raise your voice to me, young man." Shackleton purposefully clenched both fists. "I could make life very difficult for you."

"Is that a threat?" Ash stood his ground. "I'll ask you a second time to get off my property."

Shackleton refused to move.

"I know something that will prove Dino's mine," the girl blurted out, leering at me, ready to score points. "He has a white mark under his tail shaped like a maple leaf. He's had it since he was born."

She jutted her chin out defiantly and watched the flood of fear in my eyes.

"Get out," I yelled, my voice grating in the back of my throat. "It's lies, all lies – just get out before we call the police ourselves."

I was shuddering with shock. This was supposed to be one of the best days of my life. Instead this obnoxious girl was trying to ruin it.

Shackleton at least had the good sense to retreat towards the car, the girl reluctantly following. Barney stampeded round his stable, trickles of sweat breaking out on his shoulder. His eyes were fixed on the girl's back. I could see his confusion, I could see him remembering.

The Range Rover crunched out of the drive, the tyres kicking up gravel, reflecting Shackleton's

14

temper. Ash was curling up the edge of a business card flicking it between finger and thumb. Camilla wrapped an arm round my shoulders and we went into the common room so obviously shellshocked.

Cam immediately put the kettle on, flicking back her blonde hair and clanking tins looking for tea bags. My brain was whirring and I slouched in a chair biting on my bottom lip to stem the tears.

"Alex, listen to me!" Ash dragged me up, his hands unintentionally digging into the soft flesh on my inner arms. "Barney is not stolen. He's not going anywhere! It's all some dreadful mistake. Listen to me!"

I was shaking my head back and forth, blocking out his words. I'd read enough pony magazines to know that the original owner had first claims. If you bought a stolen pony then it was just tough luck.

"Alex?"

"Oh yeah?" I suddenly found my voice. "Well explain to me why Barney recognized her then. He's never been like that with anybody. He normally pulls a face, not falls into their arms. He was carrying on like *Lassie Come Home*."

I didn't mean to shout but Ash always looked on the positive side. I wanted to be realistic, I wanted to prepare myself for the very worst.

Ash pulled me into his arms, resting his chin on my head and then pressing his lips to my

15

temple. "I'll never let anybody take Barney away from you. I promise."

I didn't mention the white smattering of hairs underneath Barney's tail. Only somebody who had groomed him and cared for him with love and adoration could know about that. Whoever that girl was, she knew Barney, I was sure of that. And Sid Shackleton knew it too.

CHAPTER THREE

We didn't hear any more that night. My parents insisted it must all be a misunderstanding and my mother packed me off to bed with a mug of hot chocolate and an assurance that everything would be all right.

The next morning I was up at five o'clock to help Ash take Dolly to Burghley. It was one of those lovely dewy September mornings and as I mucked out Barney's stable I found it difficult to take Sid Shackleton's threats seriously. There must be hundreds of dun 14.2 ponies in the country. There had to be some logical explanation.

Ash already had Dolly bandaged and rugged up and she was tucking into a huge hay net. Her delicate flea-bitten grey coat never really shone but she did look as pretty as a picture and every muscle was lean and toned giving the perfect outlook of an eventer.

Zoe and Camilla were going on the Pony Club bus to see the second day of dressage, but I was going with Ash in the horsebox because Judy, the head groom, was having a day off to visit her mother in Brighton. Barney was seriously sulking when he realized he was spending another day in his stable.

The traffic was horrendous as we got caught up in the early-morning rush and then Ash decided to turn off and take a short cut through the market town of Stamford and we got hopelessly lost. We ended up having to do a ten-point turn in the middle of a lane and ask a couple of sixty-year-old joggers the way to the horse trials.

I was already tingling with excitement. Unlike yesterday, this time we were going into the stabling area and rubbing shoulders with the big boys. I could tell Ash was nervous because he was drumming his fingers constantly on the steering wheel and when I spotted the Australian riders he insisted he'd never heard of them and scowled when I joked I'd been chatting them up.

"Well after all, darling, it is what you do best."

Dolly quivered with anticipation as I led her down the ramp and waited to be shown to an empty stable. One of the bandages had worked loose and she'd been biting at the front of her rug, which had cost a fortune. Ian Stark strolled past looking ultra relaxed and professional.

The Young Eventer of the Future wasn't particularly well promoted but it was a good class to be in and Ash said it would give Dolly fantastic experience without putting any miles on the clock.

Basically it was more like a working hunter class with dressage and jumping.

I set to work with the body brush and the stable rubber and tried to focus on being a good groom. We were due in the main ring in an hour and a half. Ash plodded back from the secretary's tent, stony faced and carrying a number and a test sheet. "You're not going to believe this." He raked a hand back through his hair. "Sid Shackleton's the judge – there's no point even going in!"

"It's his job to be objective." I was desperately trying to keep up Ash's flagging spirits.

He was warming up Dolly in the collecting ring. She was shortening her stride and swishing her tail every time Ash asked for a transition. He had his long legs wrapped round her and every now and then dropped the inside rein to check she wasn't leaning. Invariably she was.

A gorgeous chestnut extended past us and then went into a superb half pass right across the arena. Ash's face dropped like a ton of bricks.

Camilla shot across from the trade stands gasping for breath to announce that Aaron, the potential deep-sea diver, had teamed up with Jasper Carrington, the local flirt with excessively rich parents, and they were guzzling Bollinger in the champagne tent using Mr Carrington's American Express card. "Do something, Alex, he's

19

not used to alcohol. A Babycham gives him a migraine."

I caught a quick glimpse of Mrs Brayfield wearing a hat that looked like an ex-parrot and then saw Zoe in pink hipsters wrestling with two of the juniors, who were brandishing water pistols and trying to duck under her arm. The Sutton Vale Pony Club had a reputation for being the worst behaved club in the country and it looked as if we were doomed to keep it.

"What do you think I can do?" I hissed, clutching on to Dolly's brushing boots. "Can't you see I've got a job to do? Honestly, Camilla, this is one boyfriend you're going to have to sort out by yourself."

Dolly cantered into the dressage arena not really giving her best but still looking dazzlingly good. She halted at X and then started her test with Ash concentrating so hard he looked in another world.

Dolly had a way of moving which was stunning to watch. She was so fluid and graceful it was poetry in motion, and nobody watching her could possibly mark her down for poor action. It was difficult to see Sid Shackleton because the judges were sitting in a special box at the far end, and the way the light was falling they were just shadows. She extended across the diagonal from F to H and moved into working canter. The test lasted approximately six minutes. I was suddenly aware that I had my fingers crossed so tight they'd gone white. Cam had disappeared and an American had taken her place with a stomach like Mount Everest and a camera slung round his neck. "Gee, honey, that's some hoss you've got there."

I watched the perfect halt and salute to finish and then Ash rode out at A on a loose rein looking absolutely gorgeous with the sun picking out his natural blond streaks and the black top hat giving him a serious sombre look.

It had been brilliant. We all knew it. I stuffed Dolly with mints as Ash dismounted and watched for the scoreboard. It was a special electronic digital thing which was easy to see. I walked Dolly round trying to quash my nerves. A glamorous bay with four white stockings swished into the arena with a poker-faced rider sitting ramrod-stiff.

Come on, Ash, you've got to win this – it will make Dolly's career. If I could have crossed my eyes and ears I would have done. Dolly belonged to a rich eccentric called Sir Charles and her previous rider, Jack Landers, had treated her really badly. When we found her she was raw with whip marks and her nerves shattered. Ash had gently coaxed her back to health and she was proving to be one of the best horses he had ever had.

Ash loosened her girth. I didn't know where

21

to put myself. Suddenly the small black screen flashed and the orange figures took shape. There was a gasp from the crowds. Ash went white. There must have been some mistake. The figures were in the fifties – that test should have been around the twenty-five mark, it was brilliant.

"What the hell's going on?" Ash thrust Dolly's reins into my hand and stormed off up the side of the arena.

"Ash, come back, wait."

The dark bay in the ring took one look at Ash and completely missed his cue for canter and then stumbled badly. Ash was running on pure white-hot anger. Losing all sense of reason myself I charged after him, dragging Dolly behind me who picked up on all the tension and started trembling like a puppy. I could see an official striding towards us out of the corner of my eye.

"Ash!" My voice came out like a squeak. There was no way I could keep up with his long legs. Sometimes you can just sense an impending disaster and I knew this was going to be a classic. "Ash!"

He ripped open the door on the small white wooden hut with the open front and Shackleton almost fell out quivering like a jelly.

"You mongrel." Ash grabbed him by the shirt collar and rammed him back against the hard wooden side. Shackleton's washy baggy eyes rolled as if they were going to fall out. At six foot one and solid muscle, Ash was no pushover.

"Get your hands off me, you stupid fool." Shackleton tried to shrug him off but Ash's hands were frozen on his shirt. I could see the muscles pulsing in his neck and down his arms. Ash abhorred violence and I know he had no intention of hurting Shackleton. He just didn't know his own strength.

People were crowding round, springing up from nowhere and pushing forwards. Dolly lurched back on the reins nearly popping my right arm out of its socket. Her eyes rolled in panic and before I could do anything to stop her she crashed back into the bonnet of a car and literally sat on it with her haunches.

I was so petrified I couldn't speak but it must have only been seconds and then she righted herself and slid off. The car was perfectly all right apart from the Mercedes emblem which was bent backwards. Dolly stood with her feet splayed and her neck stretched so low that her head was little more than a foot above the ground.

At the same moment everyone noticed Sid Shackleton slumped on the ground rubbing at his jaw and spluttering up at Ash who was standing with both fists clenched.

"H-he hit me." Shackleton scrabbled to find his feet, prodding at his jaw which was spongy

23

and unmarked. The fat American bent down to help him, the camera swinging dangerously and nearly clunking into his head.

"He's lying." Ash's eyebrows arched up in horror. "I never laid a finger on him!"

"He did so!"

Nobody seemed to have seen anything. Everybody had been watching Dolly. The steward in a suit and a bowler hat pushed forward and tried to take in the scene. Ash came across to Dolly, placing his hands on her neck and gently calming her, somehow sending reassuring vibes which I couldn't do. I'd checked her hind legs and there was no sign of injury, although swelling could set in later.

"The lad should be locked up." The American was dusting down Shackleton's coat and Shackleton was milking every minute of it. "There must be somebody here who saw him hit me. He's practically dislocated my jaw."

For somebody who'd supposedly just been thumped in the mouth he didn't have any problem talking.

"I assure you, sir, I never touched him." Ash turned to the steward appealing to his better nature. "He tripped and fell – he's making all this up."

Ash was fighting a losing battle. The steward

was obviously siding with Shackleton. And so, by the looks of it, was everybody else.

"Ash would never hurt anybody except in defence," I blurted out, stroking Dolly's muzzle whose nostrils were flared salmon pink, still breathing hard.

The steward's raggy ferret-like face gathered up like a blackening cloud. He wasn't having any of it. "Ash Burgess." He stared at Ash with tightening eyes. "You've been a disgrace to your sponsor and your sport. This will have to go to the Horse Trials Committee. But I don't mind telling you," and he leant forward a step as if to prove he wasn't frightened of Ash, "you'll be suspended for the rest of the season."

"Suspended?" I was horrified. It was worse than I thought. Ash leaned against the horsebox with his face in his hands. "The press will have a field day," he groaned. "It'll be plastered all over *Horse and Hound*."

I didn't remind him that the American had been snapping pictures of us right the way through.

"This could ruin me." He drew in his breath sharply as another thought obviously slammed into his brain. "What on earth am I going to tell Sir Charles?"

The fact that he might take Dolly away was

just too heart-wrenching to even contemplate. I wrapped my arms around his waist and clung so tight I could feel his chest rising and falling. Whatever happened I would stick by him. We were in this together. And after all, wasn't that what love was all about?

The Sutton Vale Pony Club made a worse exhibition of themselves than usual and Mrs Brayfield insisted this was the last Burghley trip in her lifetime. Everything was going all right until the end of the afternoon when everybody was supposed to meet back at the coach. Somehow half the Sutton Vale ended up on the Rossington-Field coach from Wales and a fight broke out over rugby and Will Carling of all things. One lad lost a tooth and a girl nicknamed Spanner had a pot noodle poured over her head. Mrs Brayfield lost her dead parrot hat under the driver's seat and by the time everybody got on the right coach two people were sick from too much pizza and ice cream.

Jasper Carrington sloshed out of the champagne tent at 4.30 supporting a paralytic Aaron who, apart from crashing into the model horse stall, had insisted they gatecrash the members' tent because there was something he wanted to ask Captain Mark Phillips.

I spent most of the afternoon walking Dolly

round, letting her have some grass and generally unwind. Ash wanted her to be as calm as possible before we set off home. She wasn't the world's best traveller and even with a sweat rug she more often than not ended up drenched through.

Zoe and Cam had spent most of the day at the collecting ring eyeing up the talent and offering any assistance they could. A French rider let them lead round his stallion and offered them a holiday in Provence which they sensibly turned down.

Cam had come with her mother in their Range Rover so they could have a glorified picnic with the county set, perched on fold-up chairs with bottles of wine and buckets of food trying not to speak with their mouths full or leave any litter. Cam hated it but her mother caught up with her by the Harrods store after spending an arm and a leg on Christmas presents, and there was no escape.

I managed to count fifteen different breeds of dog and at least twenty-seven labradors. Ash was in a daze and desperately trying to get in touch with Sir Charles who was at a polo tournament in Monaco. His mobile phone was permanently engaged. I gave Dolly a small feed of coarse mix, and bandaged up her legs, which now

27

took just seconds. When I first started I had to re-roll the bandage three times.

Ash was piling the tack into the horsebox which Sir Charles had provided and which had room for six horses and living accommodation. It even had a shower although the loo was a pain because everybody used it but nobody wanted to empty it. The cab was a glittering array of rosettes from all over the country and abroad. Ash never admitted it but the horsebox was his pride and joy.

I was just finishing in Dolly's compartment when I saw Camilla charging across the parking area going hell for leather and waving at Ash desperately trying to get his attention. Some other crisis concerning amorous Aaron no doubt. Perhaps he'd conked out unconscious in the members' tent.

I climbed down the four steps to the ground and knew as soon as I saw her close up that something was terribly wrong. She was heaving for breath, resting her hands on her knees, and fighting to express what she obviously had to tell us.

"It's your mum," she croaked at me. "She's been trying to get through for ages. That's why she rang us."

A cold sliver of fear prickled at my neck as I imagined car crashes and hospitals and worse.

"You'd better get back there straight away."
Cam stood up straight, wiping her mouth with
the back of her hand. "It's Barney, and that girl
Claire. She's called in the police!"

CHAPTER FOUR

There was a swarm of people round Barney's stable as we pulled into the yard. My mother came running across, her hair, usually gelled neat, wafting in all directions.

"Oh Alex, Ash, the police have been here for ages. They're talking about lawyers and everything."

I had decidedly non-horsy parents but they loved Barney and I knew this would upset them.

"Your dad's in a meeting in Preston." My mother rested her arm on mine. "He says not to panic. Eric's staying with his auntie Mary in Cornwall. I don't know what we're going to do!"

Barney was in the stable next to George, a big grey with huge feet and a Roman nose, who obviously couldn't understand what all the fuss was about.

Barney whickered as soon as he saw me, and leaned forward against a police officer who was holding his head collar. His lovely custard-yellow face registered confusion and then he took a step back and turned to the girl who was causing all this heartache. She was wearing jeans and an old

Oasis sweatshirt with trainers and her hair slicked back which made her look more boyish and tougher than before.

I don't think I'd ever hated anybody as much as I did at that moment. "How dare you?" I spat out the words. "You ought to be locked up – you're a mental case."

She winced and lowered her eyes and then rallied, putting a possessive arm on Barney's withers. "This is my Dino. I love him, and now I've found him after all this time. I'm not going to let him go."

"Now now, girls, let's not let this get out of hand." The police officer bristled with anxiety, obviously not used to horses or to situations like these.

"Barney is not going anywhere." Ash blocked the doorway, a hand resting on each side of the frame.

His strength made me feel better, but not for long.

"I've got proof." The girl curled up the corners of her mouth in a victorious smile. "Everything I need, it's just a matter of time."

A terrible listless hollow settled in the bottom of my stomach as I examined the papers. We'd moved out into the common room and most of the livery owners who'd been crowding round had gone off back to their horses.

I sat down on a plastic chair looking at photographs of Claire with Barney riding bareback, leading him down a road, wrapping her arms around his neck. And then there were registration papers. I could hardly believe it. Barney was registered with the Connemara Society. His mother was called Wheatcroft Angelic Delight and his father was an Arab called Dinerella. He'd been bred in Wales, born on the 13th May eight years ago and registered simply as Dino. At the twentieth time of looking I had to admit all Barney's markings fitted his registration papers. And then there were the white markings under Barney's tail which Claire had known about.

When I finally spoke my voice was fainter than air. "I – I – I don't know . . ."

Ash butted in, pushing back a fall of blond hair from his brow as he spoke. "We've got no comment. This is a matter for the courts to decide. But a few measly papers don't prove ownership."

Claire leapt up in a flurry of emotion, saying we couldn't keep denying the truth for ever. The police officer remained as calm as a judge and said he'd want us all down at the station to take statements. My mother burst into tears when she realized the possible costs of a court case and said she'd have to remortgage the house.

"Barney is worth a lot of money." Ash levelled his gaze at Claire, who seemed to be buckling. "He's been in the local papers regularly for a year and you say you only live thirty miles away. It seems pretty odd to me that it's taken you all this time to come forward."

Claire opened her mouth and then faltered and right on cue Sid Shackleton's Range Rover crunched into the yard. He blundered out, his face bilious black with temper and insisted Claire left immediately. "I told you not to call the police," he hissed, frogmarching her back to the car. "You could have ruined everything."

He completely ignored Ash and treated the police officer with disdain. "Any questions you need to ask, I'll be at my house." He pushed Claire into the passenger seat. "I'm acting on her behalf."

Ten minutes later when the police officer had disappeared, I mechanically answered Ash's mobile phone while he unloaded Dolly. The crackling and static on the line made it nearly impossible to hear but the booming authoritative voice was unmistakable. It was Sir Charles. "What on earth is going on?" he pounded down the line. "I've just had Sid Shackleton on the blower to say Ash has been suspended for assault."

"It's really not that bad, Sir Charles." My voice faded to a whisper.

"What? What was that, girl?"

I started crying then as I remembered Barney

charging riderless through a marquee when we'd first met Sir Charles. My darling beautiful Barney.

"Alex, get that boyfriend of yours sorted out. I'm flying over. Alex? Are you listening to me?"

I mumbled "yes" between sobs but it was too late. The line had gone dead.

"It could drag on for months." I was sitting in Ash's parents' kitchen drinking tea, syrupy with sugar, while Ash insisted on frying up some bacon and eggs on an Aga which had a mind of its own.

My eyes prickled with tears and I just didn't think I could cope. Losing Barney would be like chopping off an arm or a leg. I would never be the same again. My mother had gone home to feed the cat and wait for my dad, and Ash had finally got in touch with Eric who'd been at a tearoom all afternoon with his aunt Mary.

"Don't rely on lawyers," he bawled, raging like a madman. "We've got to do our own detective work. That Sid Shackleton is as slimy as a pit of snakes. Get in touch with the girl you bought him off – quick before Shackleton gets his slimy paws on her. Alex, are you listening? I'm driving up immediately. I'll be there in four hours." The line clicked off.

I sat cradling the mug of tea in my hands staring down at a runny egg wondering why this had to happen to me. I'd read photo stories about this kind of thing in pony magazines, but you never ever think it's going to happen to you. It's always some remote story, far away, highly improbable.

Ash pulled away my plate and gathered me up into his arms, kissing my forehead with such tenderness it sent a tremble right through my body. "My little star." He lifted up my chin, his eyes so vivid blue I wanted to dive into them to escape. "Alexandra Johnson, whatever happens, whatever it takes, I will not let anyone take Barney away from you. I promise you." He held me so tightly I could feel his ribs against mine. "Now what's wrong with my runny egg?"

Eric descended on us along with his dog Daisy precisely five hours later, cursing and complaining about bad drivers and clutching a jar of plum jam which wasn't going to do much to help our cause. I'd been home to talk to my dad and he was going to get straight on to sorting out some kind of legal help. My mother had gone to bed with a migraine but had made up a batch of Barney's favourite flapjack and stacked it in an empty ice cream carton.

"Persistence." Eric thumped his fist on the arm of his wheelchair, a wisp of steel grey hair flopping forward. As usual he was absolutely immaculate in a shirt and tie and tweed jacket.

This was the man who'd turned Barney from an out of control maniac into a top class eventer. I owed him everything.

"Ash, what have you found out?"

Daisy plonked herself down by my feet, dribbling over my Milton socks and chewing on a toy frog. Daisy was a basset hound and Barney's best friend. They adored each other and Barney always performed best when Daisy was sitting at the ringside with Eric offering moral support. Half the time she was either asleep or sucking on her favourite sausage rolls, but I suppose friendship was just being there for each other, like Ash and Eric were for me now.

Susan Hamilton, the girl that used to own Barney, said she'd bought him from a horse sale and that's all she could tell us. In fact she was less than helpful.

Ash put down a pen and notepaper. "I've arranged a meeting for tomorrow morning at 10.30."

"What about this girl Claire? We need to know everything about her: where does she come from, how long's she been working for Shackleton, why is he helping her? We need to know what's really going on. We need to know why Barney cares so much for her."

A stab of jealousy went through me but I swallowed hard and tried not to let it show. I felt as if Barney had betrayed me. It was stupid but true. I pulled at Daisy's long ears and pressed her velvety coat next to mine. I had one of the strongest-minded, most eccentric men in the country helping me, as well as a ton of emotional support from my boyfriend. If it came to a court case, I could cope. I had to.

Sir Charles burst into the house after landing at a local airstrip and getting a taxi to the yard. He was still wearing his South of France white trousers and blazer and looked totally unsuitable for a chilly autumnal evening in England.

Daisy started howling and Ash visibly shrunk back from the best sponsor he'd ever had and the man who was holding his life in the palm of his hand.

Sir Charles was built like Giant Haystacks with a fuzzy crop of red hair which made him look like a yeti. He took one look at Ash and then clasped him by the hand, pumping his elbow up and down.

"I don't care what you've done, I'll stand by you. You can keep Dolly and the horse wagon, but I've got to know – I want the truth and nothing but the truth. Did you hit him?"

Ash pulled out a chair and beckoned Sir Charles forward. "It could be a very long story."

*

Sir Charles was like a dynamo. A self-made millionaire, captain of the England polo team and now a major force in eventing, he rippled with positive energy. By nine thirty the next morning he'd hired a private detective to check out Claire Robinson and told his own personal assistant to put together a report on Sid Shackleton. "You've got to know what you're up against. Research is the basis of any successful venture. That's why most people go to the wall. They don't put in enough time on what counts the most."

Ash and I were due to visit Susan Hamilton at ten thirty but in the meantime life had to go on as usual which meant exercising the horses. Eric insisted that I had to school Barney for half an hour, even though I felt like an emotional wreck and just wanted to sit in a corner and have a nervous breakdown.

Even worse he insisted on practising leg yielding which was one of my weak links and drove Barney into one of his black moods. Leg yielding consists of moving sideways and forwards at the same time, the hind legs crossing over each other. It is meant as an exercise to make the horse supple, but Barney insisted on grabbing hold of the bit and trotting off as fast as he could with his head between his knees.

Eric told me to just tackle a few steps at a time and then go straight. For a few brief seconds it all came together and felt fantastic, then Barney grabbed hold of the left rein and charged off. I felt euphoric and then remembered the video of Mark Todd leg yielding perfectly right across the arena. We were making such slow progress it was like trudging through glue.

Eric reminded me that it takes four years to school a horse to advanced dressage and I was being my usual impatient intolerable self. If only life was just normal. We then hacked down the road to a stubble field for a sedate gallop and Ash joined us on George, who thundered down the road in a Hitchcock gag as if he was Desert Orchid. George was a really good eventer but as Eric said, when it came to a scrape he couldn't get his legs out of the way fast enough and usually ploughed into the fence. He was still a class horse and Ash described him endearingly as "thick but infectious". He was such a character the yard wouldn't be the same without him.

Eric came to watch, parking his car on a grassy track and deftly manoeuvring himself into his wheelchair, being careful to place everything in the right position. When I first met Eric he hadn't been out of his house for three years. He was bitter, aggressive and he'd completely given up on life. Barney had changed all that, created an interest and a challenge. And I knew that deep down he must be going through the same dull lurching ache that I was. Without Barney our lives would crumble.

George thundered off, paddling all four legs as Ash leaned back in the saddle and tried to wheel him round. Barney pricked up his ears and started dancing sideways. Eric was grumbling that his two top riders couldn't even hold their horses steady while he started his stopwatch. He pulled the tartan blanket round his wasted legs and ordered us to do three laps at three-quarter gallop.

We bounded off, George in the lead, the stubble slushing at the horses' legs as we gathered speed down the long side of the ten-acre field. The whipping rush of air in my face flushed away anxiety and replaced it with the familiar flood of adrenalin. Horse and rider moving as one, knowing each other's thoughts – there was no feeling like it in the whole world.

I gave Barney more rein and he surged ahead with a greater effort. George was like a muck-spreader ahead, chucking up loose soil, so we had to keep our distance. I concentrated on not letting Barney get his head too low and on keeping my shoulders back. I had a habit of leaning too far forward which forced Barney onto his forehand.

Ash let George bound on and take a four-foot hedge in his stride. I was furious with him because it meant I had to yank Barney in the mouth to stop him sailing over as well. Eric suddenly

41

gave a screeching whine of his old metropolitan police whistle which he wore round his neck and drove us all mad. The Sutton Vale Pony Club had nicknamed him HQ, short for headquarters because he was so bossy. Eric always jokingly retaliated by saying he didn't mind them having an opinion as long as it was the same as his.

I turned Barney round and galloped back, leaving Ash to renegotiate the hedge. The sun was in my eyes and it was difficult to focus but I was sure another car had pulled up beside Eric. Barney sensed my anxiety and stiffened. Now the sun was blotted out by a passing cloud and I could clearly see two figures bent over Eric, looking threatening. Ash was still at the other side of the hedge. What was he up to?

Barney galloped on, eating up the ground, his long ears flicking back and forth. I could hear raised voices and now the clear shape of a boy and girl came into focus. Claire Robinson and a lad with long hair, about five foot eleven. My blood felt as if it was curdling with fear. I saw Eric's blanket fall to the ground. The lad grabbed his binoculars and lobbed them into the field. What was he going to do next? Suddenly I heard a reassuring thundering of hoofs behind me and saw George's earnest face scrabbling through the stubble, not particularly stylish but going like the clappers.

"Hold on!" Barney surged forward.

The next few minutes were pandemonium. The lad with the long hair tried to grab hold of Barney's reins but Ash was quicker and bulldozed George into his shoulder. I grasped my reins and tried to swing Barney out of Eric's way; he had one of his wheels stuck in a rut and couldn't move.

"Yer ruddy horse thieves," the lad yelled, making another grab for Barney. "Don't think all your snooping's going to get you off the hook. That's my girlfriend's horse."

"Graham, stop it!" Panic filtered into Claire's face and she lunged at the sleeve of his coat. "For goodness' sake, the old man's disabled."

I cringed for Eric knowing that would have upset him more than anything else.

Ash leapt off George, twisted his ankle on the rough ground and staggered to get his balance.

"Be careful!" I stood there and shrieked but nothing could prepare Ash for what was coming.

The lad lunged forward and battered Ash on the side of his jaw with a clenched fist. There was a sickening thud as his bare knuckles connected and then Ash reeled backwards, his face shuddering from the shock.

"You idiot!" Claire was practically hysterical. "You stupid gormless clown!"

But Graham had just worked up a taste for

it. His cold eyes were glistening with the thrill of the attack and he turned to Eric with an icy malice.

I kicked Barney forward moments too late as Eric's wheelchair went crashing onto its side and his limp body sprawled out onto the rough dirt.

"Interfering old git!" Graham kicked at one of the spinning wheels.

"Graham!" Claire grabbed his extended arm and dragged him towards their van.

Ash and I homed in on Eric sick with apprehension. George had galloped off with his reins sagging round his neck. I felt wooden with shock as Ash righted the wheelchair and tried to heave Eric up. The humiliation must have been terrible.

I heard the van's engine roar into life and turning back my eyes locked with Graham's. The look on his face made me want to retch. He was loving every minute. His mouth opened in a cheesy grin as he cranked down the window and called after me.

"Save a kiss for me, gorgeous – we'll be seeing you in court!"

CHAPTER FIVE

Susan Hamilton lived at number 18 down a cul-de-sac marked Portland Avenue. Ash clacked at the door knocker and stood back waiting for a response.

We were still numb from shock and Ash's jaw was throbbing even though I'd given him a packet of frozen peas to hold on the swelling. Eric was unharmed, just a little shaken and humiliated. As of yet, we hadn't told the police.

I saw the curtain twitch and then a woman came to the door. Susan's mother. We were ushered into the sitting room which was full of china horses and Dalmatian dogs.

"Susan!" Her mother shouted upstairs and then said she'd go and put the kettle on.

Just when I was beginning to think nobody was coming downstairs we heard a steady thud and a girl popped her head round the door, still wearing pyjamas and cradling a mug of something steaming. "I've told the police all I know. You're wasting your time."

She was abrupt to the point of being rude. She plonked herself on the arm of the sofa and glared at Ash who squirmed uncomfortably and rubbed at his chin.

"The thing is, we've got to prove that when your parents bought Barney he wasn't stolen. We know which horse sale you got him from but we need to know who you bought him from. Was there anything suspicious?"

She shrugged her shoulders but didn't answer.

"I know you probably don't like talking about Barney," I tried to put on my most encouraging voice, "but it's really, really important."

I remembered reading a story in the local paper about how Susan had ended up in hospital when Barney bolted down a motorway and careered into a lorry. He'd almost had a mental breakdown and she'd been off school for weeks. A few months later she pulled out of the Pony Club and nobody had seen anything of her since. I never really knew her, but she looked so different now – hardened, almost embittered.

I'd used every penny I'd saved up in the bank and bought Barney for the price of meat. It had been the most momentous day of my life. I pleated the frill on one of the cushions and mentally pleaded that she'd stop putting up brick walls.

Ash tried again. I was so tied up in knots I didn't trust myself to speak. I wanted to scream at her that my life was on the line. Without Barney

46

I was nothing, but how could she possibly understand? Instead I stayed dumb and twisted the Draylon frills tighter and tighter round my index finger.

And she carried on kicking her leg and staring into space.

The front door clanged shut and we both stood outside wondering where to go from here.

Ash put a comforting arm round my shoulders and steered me through the iron railings back to his jeep. "I hate to say this," he started, his brow creasing with apprehension, "but our little ray of sunshine, Susan Hamilton, is not speaking her mind. In other words she's been got at. Someone's warned her or paid her off."

I could feel my jaw dropping lower and lower and seriously wondered whether he'd been watching too many movies.

"You mean Graham and Claire?"

"I mean don't confuse the monkey and the organ-grinder." Ash clicked my seatbelt in place and squeezed my hand. "I'm talking about Sid Shackleton."

"So what's in it for him?" Sir Charles leaned forward, almost as if not to miss a single word his private detective was saying.

It was three days since we'd visited Susan

47

Hamilton and we'd not heard another word from the grisly Graham. We had heard that a court case was going to ensue and my mum and dad were going to support me all the way.

The private detective was rooting through his papers and my eyes nearly popped out when I saw bundles of black and white photographs of Shackleton's house and yard. They must have been taken a mile away. This was a professional operation.

"It would seriously help your case if you could find evidence that Shackleton is not the upright citizen he purports to be."

"W-what do you mean?"

I couldn't quite grasp what he was going on about.

"Well for instance, we've found out that fifteen years ago in Dublin he was involved with a doping ring at a racing yard but nothing was ever proved. If we could get some hard evidence it could make all the difference. It's like someone reporting a person for evading tax and then being caught himself. It weakens the case."

"Oh."

"Now take a look at these."

Sir Charles whipped out his spectacles and pulled the photographs closer.

"Do you notice anything?"

All the photographs were of fantastic horses,

48

working in the manege, out in the fields, using a special horse walker. Each one was immaculate and well muscled, worth thousands of pounds. There was nothing strange at all.

"I'm sorry, we've drawn a blank." Sir Charles thumped down a bundle of pictures, frustrated.

"It's so obvious most people wouldn't notice." The private detective, who had worked for Sir Charles for years and was a family friend, picked up a pen and tapped at each of the horses.

"Look again."

Sir Charles drew in his breath as the penny dropped. I was still none the wiser.

"Every single horse is the same colour, a dark bay with no white marks, and all roughly the same build. All apart from this one which is a grey and I checked out belongs to one of the working pupils."

I could feel my eyes widening like saucers. "But perhaps he likes that colour." My voice sounded really lame. I knew three people in the Pony Club who always had the same colour ponies.

"He's a businessman. He buys and sells for profit, there's no room for sentiment. I think you'd agree, Sir Charles, that there's something odd going on here."

"Meaning?" I was bursting with impatience to find out.

"Meaning there could be some kind of racket going on. In fact I'm pretty sure there is, but as to what, I don't know. Yet."

Sir Charles smoothed back his rusty hair, obviously as befuddled as I was.

"I'll need more staff and a person to go in on the inside." The detective stood up clicking the locks on his briefcase.

Sir Charles shook his hand in his usual pumping fashion.

"Good work, Jason, and remember time is of the essence. We're all working against the clock."

"No problem, sir, but if I may just suggest – you should fit up an extra alarm system around that pony of yours. These kind of conditions build up emotions like a pressure cooker. Anybody could suddenly decide to do anything. We wouldn't want another Shergar on our hands."

The word Shergar made my blood feel as if it had been replaced by ice water. A racehorse who had been kidnapped, never to be seen again. And that could happen to Barney.

Ash's appointment with the Horse Trials Committee clashed with a lecture he was supposed to be giving to the Sutton Vale juniors on tack cleaning. Eric put me up for the job saying it would take my mind off everything and keep my brain in gear.

Days were flying past like confetti and all we'd been able to find out was that Claire had definitely been seen with a dun pony about two years ago and a couple of the neighbours where she used to live in Ashington swore that it was the same pony as in the picture we showed them. It wasn't looking good. In fact it was looking downright terrible. How could I eat or function properly with this hanging over my head?

The last thing I felt like doing was trying to grope my way through a talk on tack cleaning to a bunch of fidgeting seven to thirteen year-olds. Zoe and Camilla were no help at all and my mind just kept whizzing back to Ash standing in front of a bunch of old dinosaurs pleading his innocence when Shackleton had probably bought them all off anyway.

Zoe and Camilla were going to watch eventing videos and discuss Eric's birthday plans. Just as I expected, Jasper, Aaron, Spanner and some of the others turned up armed with pizza and a pile of action films. So much for Zoe's good intentions of studying olympic gold medallist Blythe Tait . . .

A horde of the worst-behaved kids turned up crammed in Camilla's mother's Range Rover and then Mrs Brayfield followed in her new Golf.

I frantically scoured my notes again even

though I'd been cleaning saddles and bridles since the year dot.

Stubborn balls of grease and dirt known as jockeys can be removed carefully with a blunt knife. Every time you clean your saddle, swap over the stirrup leathers. This stops them stretching unevenly as a result of mounting on one side.

Dip the bar of saddle soap into a bucket of clean water and rub it over your soaping sponge. Never dip the sponge into the water and rub it on the soap, as you'll end up with a foaming mess.

That's when my handwriting started to deteriorate. A MATCHSTICK OR COCKTAIL STICK IS GREAT FOR GETTING RID OF SOAP THAT'S CLOGGING UP BUCKLE HOLES. That was Ash's writing – in capital letters.

"Cooee!" Mrs Brayfield marched into the common room where I'd set out various bits of bridles and leather girths and cleaning sponges.

Judy, the head groom, had insisted on taking out a couple of the four year-olds for a hack because she was too worried about Ash to hang around the yard, which left me by myself.

Everybody piled into the common room and immediately homed in on the pool table which was pushed up against the back wall and was Ash's pride and joy. Unfortunately I hadn't packed away the balls and the cues and within seconds the white ball was pinging off the table and scooting across the room at a hundred miles an hour. They soon settled down and I talked and demonstrated for an hour. I had just finished taking questions, when I heard a horse come into the yard. It was Judy.

Ash's jeep crunched into the yard behind her. He looked tense and his hands were fixed to the wheel. It had all gone off quicker than we'd expected. He was still in his suit but had pulled off his tie and slung it across the dashboard.

Judy jumped off the skittish liver chestnut and led both horses across to us eager to know one way or the other. Ash's face said it all. He slammed the car door shut, shrugged his shoulders and went straight over to Donavon's stable. I trotted after him not knowing whether to ask him outright or wait for him to tell me.

Donavon was a beautiful 16.2 bright chestnut with an almost regal expression, a real gentleman. He snorted enquiringly as Ash just stared at me, running one finger down the powerful shoulder muscle and watching the skin quiver.

Donavon was the best horse in Ash's string, an advanced eventer just coming into his peak.

Ash had brought him up through the grades, nursing and nurturing his amazing talent. His whole career had been angled towards Badminton next spring.

I was terribly worried about what Ash might tell me – that he'd been suspended and would miss a qualifying competition in two weeks.

He slowly turned round and we swapped a smile that neither of us could make convincing. It was the worst, I just knew it.

"Well, baby, it looks as if you might not be going anywhere for a very long time." Ash soothed Donavon's neck with the flat of his hand.

"You've been suspended?" My mouth had gone dry.

"There's something I want you to do for me." Ash levelled a gaze at me so intense it made my stomach flutter. I had no idea what was coming. It was the very last thing I expected. And it made my heart do a triple somersault.

"I want you to ride Donavon for me – professionally. Give him a chance to prove himself. And you, I know you can do it. So what do you say, Alex? Will you ride him?"

CHAPTER SIX

The big breakthrough came early the next morning and was all down to Sir Charles' private detective.

There was a lady called Mrs Clarke who had bought a bay thoroughbred cross Hanoverian from Sid Shackleton, eight years old and a budding dressage prospect. However, as soon as she'd got the horse home he'd proved enormously disappointing and she'd embarked on a course of lessons with Shackleton which had cost a small fortune.

She was willing to talk to us and to show us her horse but she didn't want any publicity or her name mentioned in any shape or form. *Horse and Hound* had just come out that morning plastered with the story of Ash's suspension and the American's pictures of him looking down at a prostrate Shackleton with his fist clenched. There was an article on whether the ruling board should be tougher on bad behaviour and whether riders were upgrading at too young an age and the pressure was getting to them. I just hoped Mrs Clarke hadn't changed her mind and we'd be too late.

The horse was kept at a livery yard about an hour's drive away and Mrs Clarke agreed to meet us there. Sir Charles, Ash and myself all piled into the jeep and set off not really knowing what to expect or even what to ask.

It was an average establishment with lots of ponies and a grassy track worn to dust, with a few jumps spread about, all below three foot. A little boy with a grey Welsh mountain pony asked me why he always went to the wrong gate no matter how much he tried to train him not to. Three Jack Russells came hurtling round the back of a trailer and developed a fascination with Sir Charles' trousers, pulling at the hems and refusing to let go.

Mrs Clarke was down at the far end in one of the modern loose boxes. A girl with a stud in her nose pointed out which stable and implied that Mrs Clarke was nice but slightly crackers. She sounded very much like Jenny, one of our livery owners who had a horse called Gypsy Fair who was the equine equivalent of a hypochondriac.

It wasn't what we wanted to hear.

The horse was beautiful. A lovely powerful glistening bay with an intelligent head and a gentle temperament. Unfortunately once she was tacked up and out on the grass track she moved as flat as a pancake. The mare hadn't got any action at

56

all. I couldn't understand how she could possibly have been sold as a dressage horse. It is essential to have free-flowing action in all paces and this mare was as stiff as a board. Mrs Clarke didn't help matters by taking too firm a hold and tweaking the reins erratically every time she asked for a transition. Ash groaned and Sir Charles said we must hear her out.

Eventually she came bundling back to us, her arms flapping in an effort to get more impulsion.

"I've had over a hundred lessons," she rasped, "and we still can't even do a decent novice."

Inexperienced riders are always advised to buy schoolmaster horses to give them confidence but this mare called Saffy didn't seem to have any class at all.

"Would you mind me asking how much you paid for her?" Sir Charles shuffled his feet, obviously having similar thoughts.

"Seven thousand nine hundred pounds with a dressage saddle thrown in."

We all gasped in amazement. Saffy was a nice hack but not worth any more than two thousand. Mrs Clarke had been taken to the cleaners.

"She's won an intermediate class and qualified for Goodwood. Mr Shackleton showed me the rosettes. She's got BHS points."

Ash arched his eyebrows at me as Saffy

slumped onto three legs, resting a fourth. Ash examined her teeth to check that they corresponded with her age and Mrs Clarke dismounted and pulled the reins over her head.

"Would you mind if I tried her out?" Ash stepped forward, ready to lengthen the stirrups.

Saffy woke up as Ash clicked her into trot and improved enormously as he worked her on both reins, pushing into canter and then asking for a direct halt, moving on again and trying to set her up for half pass.

Eventually he rode back to us on a loose rein, his mouth puckered up in concentration. "There's no way this horse could perform an intermediate test. She doesn't know what extension is, or leg yielding. She's completely green."

Sir Charles glanced at Mrs Clarke as if expecting to find an explanation.

"Well, isn't it obvious?" she snapped impatiently, tucking back a tuft of salt-and-pepper hair under her riding hat. "This is not the horse I originally bought."

"It's too unbelievable for words." Sir Charles soaked his greasy spoon breakfast in tomato sauce and wiped the knife and fork on his jacket.

We'd stopped at a transport café, to gather our thoughts and fill up on sausage, bacon and eggs.

"So let me get this right." I tried to make sense of it for the twentieth time. "Sid Shackleton has a top class intermediate horse up for sale which he cons beginner riders into buying. And then when they come to collect him he swaps the good horse for a lookalike dud which nobody would guess wasn't the same horse. Then when they ring up to complain he insists it's their bad riding and sells them a course of exclusive lessons. So he's making money all round."

"And that's why all his horses are the same colour, build and breed." Ash stabbed at a stray sausage.

"With no white marks!" I cradled my coffee cup to warm my hands, surreptitiously slipping all the sugar lumps into my pocket for Barney.

"It's too bizarre for words. For heaven's sake, the man's a respected judge, in charge of the junior team."

"But he's still after making a good living," I added, "and horses are notorious for getting people into debt. Maybe he's trying to pay off a big bank loan or something."

"Whatever he's doing, he's a crook and a liar and a cheat." Ash rubbed at his jaw in trepidation. "Somehow we've got to set a trap, get all the proof we need. I'm sure that if we blow his cover it will all work out with Barney."

Sir Charles paid the bill and ushered us out

of the swing doors. "That head groom of yours . . ." Sir Charles graciously opened the door of the jeep for me, pushing up a pile of coats.

"Judy?" I answered, thrown off balance.

"The pretty one with the blonde hair . . . I think it's time I got to know her better."

Judy Richards was eighteen with natural blonde hair which she lightened and a fairish skin dotted with freckles. She was glamorous and good fun and her ambition was to groom at the Olympics, hopefully with Ash. When I'd first brought Barney to the yard she had been seeing Ash and they were quite an item. It took months for us to become friends after Ash swapped camps and starting dating me.

As head groom she held the yard together and acted on Ash's behalf when he was away competing. There were thirty-two horses stabled at the yard. Some were Ash's eventers and the others were liveries. It was a seven day a week, twenty-four hour a day job and Ash was always on the lookout for more part-time help, the cheaper the better.

And so would be Sid Shackleton.

Judy had guts, I'll give her that, but the thought of what Sir Charles was proposing made her visibly quake.

"He'll know for sure, I'm bound to give the game away."

"Not if you're partly honest." Sir Charles had it all worked out. "You tell him you were Ash's head groom but you're sick and tired of his arrogance and poor wages for long hours. You wanted to get back at him and this was the perfect way."

"But what if he sees through me?"

"He won't. His ego is so big he'll love the idea of getting one over on Ash. Trust me. It will work."

The plan was for Judy to go into Shackleton's yard as a groom so she could keep an eye on what was going on. If we could catch him redhanded we'd be able to call in the police. Also Judy's brief was to get close to Claire, who was a working pupil and lived in a flat above the stables. Up to now Sir Charles' team hadn't been able to find out anything about her that was suspect. She'd lived with her parents, done well at school and worked at a local riding school. Everybody we'd spoken to had backed up the story that she rode a dun pony although she didn't keep it at the riding school. It had been reported stolen and scores of people remembered Claire being terribly upset and losing a lot of weight.

The whole business then just seemed to fizzle out. Until, that is, she went to work for Shackleton and he obviously told her about

61

Barney and encouraged her to follow it up. But why would he be so interested in helping her? What was in it for him? Surely something?

The net was closing in. It seemed inevitable that Barney would be reclaimed as a stolen pony. But I knew I could never let that happen. No matter what the cost.

Judy must have been reading my thoughts. "I'll do it to try and befriend Claire and get to the bottom of it, but I don't want any funny business with Shackleton. He's a power freak. To be honest he scares me."

Zoe insisted I go for a ride with her the following morning as she said Lace needed bags more exercise and she needed all the practice she could get now she'd decided to be a mounted police officer. Last week it had been an actress and the week before that an interior designer. Some morbid thought at the back of my head told me to ride Barney as much as I could while I still had the chance.

It was a beautiful fresh morning and Barney strode out almost jauntily, listening for the slightest command to quicken his pace. As soon as I was in the saddle I felt heaps more positive and made the most of all the stubble fields and the opportunity to jump a few dykes.

Zoe screeched at the top of her voice as Lace

cat-leapt over a drainage ditch and nearly lost her footing at the other side. Lace was a lovely 14.2 grey with a pretty face, but not very bold. But what she lacked in cross-country she made up for in dressage.

Zoe sauntered along a nearby hedge, her feet out of the stirrups, pulling off plump blackberries and then cursing when the purple juice leaked all over her cream jodhpurs.

We were both competing tomorrow in the Sutton Vale Pony Club Hunter trials, and Eric insisted on business as usual. I was entered for the open class and Zoe for the novice. My main competition was Jasper on Star and Camilla on her pony, The Hawk, but recently she'd been spending far too much time with Aaron, and The Hawk had just been hacked out with Judy and had no jumping practice at all.

We were supposed to be taking our Pony Club C-plus test but I really didn't know whether I had the heart for it. Zoe practised riding with one hand and then asked me how many gallons a horse drank a day. There were loads of questions on stable management and it was quite a difficult test to be taking at fifteen.

A pheasant flew up from the hedgerow and Barney skittered sideways. I let him bound on and jump a small hedge with a rail in front.

Zoe casually let it drop that her mother was

treating her to some lessons because she thought Lace was starting to slip. Usually everyone at the yard had lessons with Ash because he was so encouraging without being critical and he could spot a problem a mile away. But what was wrong with Eric? He was our trainer and mentor.

Zoe said this time she was going somewhere else and I narrowed my eyes and pulled up Barney in a square halt.

"Well, you can't keep me in suspense," I said, sensing she'd got something up her sleeve. "Eric will be mortified."

"Oh no he won't," she answered glibly, squeezing Lace on and looking like the cat who'd got the cream. "Because it's Sid Shackleton – I'm going undercover too."

CHAPTER SEVEN

"I heard about Zoe." Ash came up behind me, clamping a hand round my waist and causing me to jump back in alarm.

My nerves were shredded enough without Ash adding to the strain. I bit my lip, though, when I saw his hurt expression and the obvious care in his eyes.

"I just wondered where you'd got to."

I was in the back field picking mushrooms and unaware of how late it was. Everybody had gone home ages ago. Ash plucked the stalk off a particularly large specimen and bit into it raw.

"I can't ride Donavon." I blurted out the words and then dropped all the mushrooms when I saw his face fall. "It just wouldn't be right."

"Why not?"

"I just can't."

He lobbed the half-eaten mushroom over towards the field gate and narrowed his eyes. I swallowed hard and tried to explain.

"It's either got to be me and Barney together or nothing at all. Don't you see, if I start riding Donavon, it's like a betrayal, it's like giving up.

And if I lose Barney, then I'm going to pack in horses, there's no point carrying on."

I didn't expect him to understand. I was staring at his long sooty eyelashes for ages before he spoke.

"You're right." His voice was gravelly and tinged with emotion. "You've got to do what you think is best. And what's right for you will be right for me. I love you, Alex Johnson, just you remember that."

He shot me a lopsided grin and then a gorgeous crinkly smile and I folded into his arms and buried my face into his rugby shirt, deeply grateful that I had such a fantastic boyfriend.

The Sutton Vale Hunter Trials was held on the Pony Club showground which was flat but made up of some really good jumps. The trouble with the lack of undulating ground was that there was nothing to slow up the horses. They tended to start at a flat-out gallop and lose control altogether halfway round, careering through the finish or setting off at a tangent over the surrounding fields.

Barney was in his usual snaffle and Grackle but Cam had The Hawk in a Pelham with double reins. I was entered in the Open which was for both horses and ponies with the jumps three foot six maximum. Ash had two novice horses entered and was going to take George round just for the fun of it to try and revive his interest. Recently he'd been clouting every practice jump in the manege and Ash had been at his wit's end to know what to do. Eric had suggested leaning two poles on a jump to form a V so that he'd be forced to jump in the middle of a fence and snap up his forelegs. It worked a treat until we took the poles down and then he just reverted back to his old ways. Ash at one stage thumped down his whip and stomped off to the common room threatening to send him to the local riding school. George just snorted and waltzed off to talk to Nigel and Reggie, the two ducks who were always in his stable.

Eric appeared looking harassed from behind the secretary's tent, a clipboard and pen balanced precariously in his lap and Daisy tugging along at his side, her extendable lead snagging on his wheels. His jaw was set rigid with the effort of pushing through the soft ground but he would never let anyone push him unless it was a matter of life and death. Ash knew better than to suggest it.

Jasper Carrington shot past on Star who was lathered in sweat and heading for the start. Zoe nearly let go of Lace as she ogled a new rider lunging a flashy bay over in the corner. Daisy bustled up to Barney and licked his pinky coloured nose, delighted to see him. The loudspeaker croaked into life as Jasper was the first to set out on the Open course, taking all the fast options. As a hunter trial course it was extremely well built, with solid fences as imposing as any BHS course.

Eric noticed my mind wandering and my spirit hovering somewhere in my boots.

"Business as usual." He thrust a list of diagrams into my hand on how to tackle the timed section. He had spent the last half an hour with his binoculars trained on the course watching how it was riding.

The timed section was made up of a log complex and tight turns doubling back which would need precision riding and bags of impulsion. We'd walked the course already and nerves were churning up my stomach. I always got nervous beforehand but somehow this time I had a feeling of dread. The potato salad I'd eaten earlier performed several backflips and I had to double over to ease the nausea.

Ash was heading down to the start on George who, although allowed to go round the course, wasn't taking part in the competition because he was over-qualified. Everywhere spectactors were casting admiring glances as the two of them sauntered past looking ultra professional, and I swelled with pride.

Cam was getting unbearably ratty as The Hawk tried to do pirouettes on her sore toe and Aaron prattled on about conservation and whether horses enjoyed being ridden. I mounted Barney and decided to warm up in the practice ring to loosen the tension. The trouble with competing on home ground was that everybody expected great things. Barney was well known in the area and as we picked our way through the streaming mass of bodies, people stopped and pointed. It was like being in a goldfish bowl.

The loudspeaker announced that Ash had set off on the course and I pulled Barney onto a higher piece of ground near the hot dog stall where I had a good view of the first half of the course.

George was going like the clappers over the barrels, log pile and palisade, checking for the first complex, a jump into shallow water with a bank on the other side. They looked fantastic together, George's glistening bay coat and Ash's green and white colours flitting through the trees. I strained my neck to catch a glimpse as they jumped into the wood and skimmed through the coffin and out on the other side towards a sloping brush.

George pushed his nose up in the air and stretched forward, taking a strong hold of the bit. Ash leaned back slightly and tried to balance him.

Then they disappeared round some trees and I couldn't see anything.

There was a groan from the crowds. The microphone crackled and then broke off. It was as if everything had suddenly gone into slow motion.

"Ash!"

George suddenly appeared from the blanket of trees galloping flat out, his reins dragging round his hoofs.

"The idiot's crash-landed!" Cam jostled up beside me, pushing The Hawk forward with frantic leg movements.

"He didn't take off!" A woman in a parka coat and a stony complexion was plucking at her husband's sleeve.

The red cross ambulance cranked into gear and as discreetly as possible pushed through the crowds at ten miles an hour.

"Ash!" Tears pricked at my eyes as I pushed Barney into a trot and caught a glimpse of Ash lying prone on the grass in front of the brush fence. There were people round him and Cam was charging after George who had got bored and had started grazing over by the water jump. Thoughts of Willie Carson ending up in intensive care and fighting for his life from a simple kick flashed through my mind. Ash could be lying there in a pool of blood hovering on the brink of death.

Eric had disappeared. So had Zoe. An official

stepped forward blocking my way with a rope saying I couldn't go any further. "But I'm his girl-friend!" I squeaked, shaking and not knowing whether it was me or Barney.

"It's concussion." A fence steward came running up to make sure the next horse hadn't been started. "I think he needs a few stitches."

"Stitches!" My mind was whirring in overdrive.

"That horse has got no brakes. Even a lad of his strength couldn't hold him."

I leapt off Barney, left him standing by the group of people and hurtled off before anybody could stop me. Cam had caught George and was leading him back to the horsebox, still riding The Hawk. At least George seemed OK.

I barged into the ambulance to find Ash sitting upright, conscious, with a doctor examining his eyes.

"I'm all right, don't panic." Ash saw the horror widening my eyes as a nurse set to work bandaging the fleshy part of his right thumb which was ripped open and gushing with blood.

"How many fingers am I holding up?" The doctor held up three fingers and Ash said "four".

The nurse came to the end of the bandage, and the doctor said he must go straight to Casu-alty for stitches and he'd have to stay in overnight for concussion. He then gave him a lecture about wearing a watch with a glass face when he was riding. The glass had smashed when he'd landed and a jagged strip had dug into his thumb. As a professional eventer Ash should have known better. He normally wore his stopwatch but because he wasn't competing seriously, he hadn't thought to change it. It was a stupid mistake and he was lucky it hadn't severed an artery.

The nurse dabbed at his forehead with a damp cloth, wiping away a streak of dust, and seemed most put out that a girlfriend had suddenly appeared on the scene.

"So what happened?" I demanded, anxious to talk horses now that I knew he was going to live. Ash looked at me rather glazed, smiled weakly and answered as honestly as he could.

"He just didn't jump. His forelegs never came up. It felt weird. I think there was something wrong with him, Alex. He didn't co-ordinate."

Ash went to hospital with Mrs Brayfield, who seemed pleased to escape from the clutches of hordes of parents and screaming kids. There was still a raging feud going on about the under-14.2 pairs and who was the rightful winner, despite the judge's decision being final.

Eric had gone in a Land Rover driven by Zoe's dad to inspect the brush fence and see if it needed to be roped off. The next competitor, who had already been waiting twenty minutes, was complaining bitterly and trying to control a black cob with a hogged mane who couldn't understand why he'd been trudging round in circles when it was obvious he was meant to be jumping.

Everyone was asking about Ash. I also got the feeling that some people were thrilled that a high-flying rider like Ash had come off when they had gone clear.

With a sudden rush of panic I remembered that I'd left Barney loose in the collecting ring when I'd dashed off to the ambulance. Boiling panic quickly simmered when I realized Cam had probably taken him back to the horsebox, along with George. It made sense. He wasn't anywhere to be seen in the collecting ring. The cream Lambourn horsebox with the red stripe was parked next to a cattle wagon and seeped in six inches of mud. Cam had the ramp down and was shaking out a Melton rug and unfolding the roller. I popped my head round the corner to see George pulling at a hay net looking quite happy with himself while The Hawk stood next to him scowling and probably wondering why he wasn't in his own trailer.

Barney always travelled in the front compartment where I could pop through the living quarters to check on him. I walked over to the groom's door to climb in.

"Where's Barney?" Cam's voice was taut and strained.

"I . . . I . . ." My own faded to a whimper when I realized my beloved Barney was not in the horsebox nor anywhere else in sight. "I thought you had him," I managed to bark. "You must have seen him. He was unmissable . . ."

Cam threw down the rug and grabbed a bucket and a head collar. "Where is he most likely to have gone?"

"Food!" I said, colour flooding back into my cheeks in a rush. "He always heads for the nearest food stall!"

"Well, he isn't at the burger bar and they've stopped serving tea and cakes."

The showground was a moving mass of cars, people and horses, but no dun 14.2 pony on the rampage.

"I'll check the course and by the secretary's tent, you do the car park and the tents." Cam shot off, a flood of blonde hair streaming out from her hairnet.

"Oh Barney, please don't have got into trouble," I half murmured, half prayed. The car park was horseless and there were no stray horses round the boxes. There was a grassy parkland area and then a clump of tents selling saddlery, showjumps and overpriced winter coats.

My chest was heaving by the time I'd raced

74

up and down the aisles and still seen no sign of
Barney. I was about to go back to the horsebox
to wait for Cam when instinct told me to nip in
between two tents and head for a van half hidden
away and lettered with KAY'S CATERING.

I knew I was on the right tracks. I half
climbed, half jumped over a pile of crates and
heard a familiar neigh. Relief gushed into my
bloodstream. There was Barney, his head buried
in a cellophane-wrapped pack of doughnuts, red
jam oozing out all over his whiskers and pink
muzzle and sticking to his knees where he'd been
rubbing his nose. His saddle was lopsided and his
Grackle noseband undone. As I stepped closer,
shouting his name, I saw somebody was round
the left side undoing his girth.

Barney's sudden confused expression made
my mouth go dry.

Claire Robinson stepped out from under
Barney's neck, her face glowering white hot with
anger. She clasped hold of my black rubber reins
and resentment shook through me like an
earthquake.

"Get away from my horse," I bawled,
wanting to claw her eyes out.

"*Your* horse, that's a joke," she hissed. "You
can't even look after him properly. You dump him
by himself where he could get knocked down by

a car and then half an hour later you decide to come and look for him."

"Well who do you think you are?" I screamed, shuddering with anger. "You haven't even got the sense to stop him eating those doughnuts."

Barney started trembling and stared guiltily at me with half a doughnut stuck to his top lip as if he knew what I was saying.

"Don't you know you're not supposed to shout near horses?" Claire backed Barney up a few steps and refixed his noseband. "You're not fit to own any horse, never mind Dino."

"How dare you?" I felt my fists clench into hard knots. "It's me who Barney loves. He was a wreck when I first got him, it's me who's turned him into something."

"Well bully for you." Claire jutted out her chin. "You stuck-up old boot, Dino's mine and he loves me – it stands out a mile."

I made a rush forward to snatch Barney's reins, but he lurched back, mistaking my intentions.

"You idiot!" Claire screeched as Barney staggered back on his haunches, half reared and then swivelled round, tearing the reins from her hand. "Look what you've done now!"

Barney suddenly realized he was free and,

rattled from all the shouting, cantered off with his tail in the air as if to teach both of us a lesson.

Claire looked as if she was going to grab me by the throat. "We'll see who he cares most about," she muttered through frozen lips. "Whoever he comes back to is the one he really belongs to. You can't get fairer than that."

My chest was banging so much I thought my ribs would smash but I couldn't back down, I wasn't going to give her the pleasure.

"You stand thirty paces to his left and I'll go to his right, and when I raise my hand, we'll start shouting."

"You're on!" I ploughed through the soft grass counting methodically, forcing myself to stay calm.

This was madness, my head was screaming at me to stop. Barney sulkily snatched at some grass and then watched us steadily as we took up our positions. I could see a few traders and mums and toddlers watching us from the saddlery tents obviously having heard all the commotion. Claire raised one hand and then started shouting at the top of her voice.

"Barney!" I leaned forward without moving my feet, desperate to get his attention. "Barney, come on boy, come on!"

"Dino! Dino!" Claire was hollaing with both hands wrapped round her mouth.

"Barney!" ... "Dino!" ... "Barney!" ...
"Dino!"

That clever, beautiful, yellow horse stood
there, befuddled, confused, hovering from one
foreleg to the other, not knowing what to do for
the best. He was like a child caught up between
two raging parents heading for the divorce courts.
How could he be made to choose between two
people he obviously cared about? Barney belonged
to no one. He was a free spirit, a special person
in his own right, and this was tacky and wrong.

I slowly turned round and walked away,
hating myself for stooping to such a level. I had
my head slung so low I nearly didn't see Eric
furiously wheeling up the field, his cheeks inflated
with rage, and Camilla trotting after him clanking
a bucket and looking like she'd just had a roas-
ting. Barney, as if he'd suddenly found an escape
route, kicked up his heels and tore after Camilla,
neighing loudly, and putting food first on the
agenda.

A bemused smile quivered at the corner of
my lips.

"There's nothing to smirk about, my girl,"
Eric thundered, as Barney careered past. "I want
the truth and nothing but the truth. What the
devil's been going on?"

CHAPTER EIGHT

"He's awful!" Judy propped up her elbows on the shiny formica top in the transport café we'd picked out as a meeting point.

She'd been working for Sid Shackleton for eleven days and she'd quickly come to the conclusion that he was a slavedriver and a male chauvinist pig. I was with Sir Charles who was getting more and more disillusioned with human nature and giving himself hernias because we couldn't pin anything concrete on Shackleton, even though we all knew he was taking everyone for a ride.

Claire's boyfriend Graham, the thug who attacked Ash, hung round the place doing odd jobs and generally acting like a louse. Judy hated him and said he chatted up all the girls in the yard and hardly gave Claire a second thought. She rolled up her shirtsleeve and showed us a fat bruise starting to yellow where he'd pinched her just for the fun of it. Everybody called him Shackleton's pet Rottweiler, only Rottweilers have more brains.

On the Claire front, things weren't going very

well. On the first day Judy had accidentally upset her by using her favourite grooming kit. Judy said she was sullen, moody and unbelievably touchy. There was as much chance of her opening up about Barney as there was of getting a confession from Shackleton. We'd just have to keep digging.

The news was much better about Shackleton. A couple from Dorset called Green had bought a horse called Red Cloud and were due to pick him up in the next three days. It was marked in the diary for three o'clock Thursday. Shackleton never let anybody but his head groom Jesse prepare a horse for its new owner. Sir Charles said he could smell a sewer full of rats and all we had to do now was prove what Shackleton was up to and call in the police.

"Easier said than done." Judy raked back her pale blonde hair and refixed a tortoiseshell clip. "He moves his horses round like musical chairs. I never know who I'm looking after next."

"Stick with it." Sir Charles pressed forward an envelope with some money, telephone numbers and a phonecard. "We'll catch the no-gooder, I know we will. And keep nagging away at Claire. If the pressure builds up too much, she might just explode and blow her story. She's telling fibs somewhere along the way and Shackleton is feeding her the lines. I could put money on it."

"Oh, and there was something else." Judy

put down her cup of coffee in excitement. "One of the other grooms, Tracey I think it was, well anyway, she said Claire had some relatives in Australia. A sister, definitely a sister – in Melbourne."

Sir Charles whipped out his notebook and jotted it down at lightning speed. Claire's parents had made a statement to verify her story, but a sister in another country might not have been briefed. She might be able to spill the beans. If we could find her . . . It would be difficult to track down a Robinson in Melbourne, and that was providing she was using her maiden name. Sir Charles told me not to be so negative and I shrugged my shoulders. What else could I be? At the moment we had almost nothing to go on.

Sir Charles grated back his chair and kissed Judy on both cheeks. We arranged to meet in two days' time at the same place. Judy couldn't ring from the yard because there were always people around and Shackleton had an itemized phone bill which recorded calls made and their numbers.

"Be careful." Sir Charles clasped her hand, staring meaningfully into her almond-shaped eyes.

None of us, at that time, had an inkling of how dangerous it was all going to become.

George stood in his stable, eyeing Ash beadily as he made a move with the bridle. His big bay head lolled up and down and then he scowled sulkily as Ash pushed a thumb in his mouth to slip in the bit.

Ever since the hunter trial George hadn't wanted to go near a fence, let alone jump one. For a horse who was usually so bold that he'd jump the side of a house, it was a definite turn-around in behaviour.

Ash had spent one night in hospital with concussion and had since been grouching around all week, riding with one hand, and scratching irritably at the stitches which were holding his thumb together. Even worse, Donavon, his star horse, had developed an abscess on the sole of his near fore which meant he couldn't be ridden for a few weeks. He was being turned out every day and had already managed to destroy two all-weather rugs. So even if Ash hadn't been sus-pended they'd be out of the qualifying competition where all the big names were making a final appearance before closing down till the spring.

Eric was coming over to take a look at George, who was fretting so badly he was even off his food. Nigel and Reggie, the two ducks, scuttled and scuffled excitedly across the arena, following George's waddling hocks. Because George was such a messy eater, he'd become flavour of the month with the ducks and Nigel in particular had developed the fine art of hoovering up every stray shred of barley.

George eyed a red and white pole and started trembling. He looked as if any minute now he'd jump into Ash's arms.

"The poor lad's completely lost his confidence." Eric always showed more sympathy for horses than he did for riders and insisted ninety-nine per cent of the time it wasn't the horse's fault.

I was ordered to go and tack up Barney while Eric insisted Ash start with some rustic poles which weren't quite so daunting.

Eric had always had a soft spot for George and was deeply offended that Sir Charles was talking about selling him if he didn't get his act together. Everyone was saying George was unpredictable, and had too much strength and not enough in the brain department. Eric intended to prove them wrong.

I gave Ash a lead over some simple two-foot jumps but as soon as Ash tried to go himself George dug in his heels, scuffing up a red cloud of sand.

"He's lost it completely." Ash neck-reined back to Eric, irritable and steamed up. "I always knew he was useless."

Eric, immaculate in striped tie and shirt and a sports jacket which faintly smelled of mothballs, had other ideas. "Take off his over-reach boots."

"What?" Ash looked thrown.

"You heard me: take off his over-reach boots

and then canter a tight circle and pop over the four-foot upright."

"You're joking."

"Just do it."

Over-reach boots are protective strips of plastic or rubber which fit around the horse's fetlock so they cover the heel area which is prone to being struck by a hind hoof. Over-reach injuries always take ages to heal so most eventers do all their jumping in these. Barney had a smart black pair.

Obeying orders, Ash yanked at the velcro strips, chucked the boots over by the gate and then vaulted back into the saddle. George didn't look any different.

Ash circled him and he popped over the four-foot fence as good as gold.

"What's going on?" We were both flabber-gasted.

Eric pulled out a shabby, ripped, mud-spattered over-reach boot from under his blanket and slung it on the sand in front of us.

"George didn't refuse that fence at the hunter trial. He accidentally stood on his boot and tripped himself up. He was going so fast he couldn't right himself in time and so obviously he's lost his nerve. Would you want to jump in a pair of boots that caused you to land on your back? I think not."

"And you found this by the fence when you went back with Zoe's dad." I fingered the ruined boot and wondered why he'd taken so long to tell Ash.

"I wanted you to work it out for yourself." Eric was being at his most arrogant and cantankerous.

"Well, thanks." Ash ripped off his suede chaps and threw them down in front of Eric. "You always have to prove you know best, don't you? No matter what, you're the better horseman. Just because you can't get up there in the saddle . . ."

"Ash, stop it." I tried to butt in.

"No, Alex, he's so full of his own importance, he makes me sick." Ash swivelled round on his heel and stomped off.

I was about to follow him but Eric snatched my arm and held me back.

"Leave him. He's furious that he's been suspended and he's just realized he's got a horse here who could win the Badminton qualifier."

"Oh," I said, slightly shocked. And we both turned round to see George lying down in the sand, gently snoring and batting his long gingery eyelashes. "Really?"

Zoe trudged out of her dad's Land Rover Discovery bow-legged with pain after her sixth lesson with Sid Shackleton. She was on a crash course

85

of intensive training and she had bags under her eyes the size of suitcases.

"Nothing," she grunted, staggering to the trailer where Lace was meekly tied up inside. "Not a dicky bird."

We were trying to get Shackleton to suggest a backhander for marking Zoe up in a dressage competition she was going to enter. But he wasn't biting.

"He knows." Zoe grasped for a can of Lucozade. "I know he does. And when we turned into the drive, there was a red Escort following us and I could put my life on it, it was that groom Jesse."

"Oh great, terrific." My nerves were twanging like guitar strings. "Isn't anything ever going to go right?"

Lace came out of the trailer looking as exhausted as Zoe and dragged at her hay net as if she hadn't seen food for a week. Zoe did exactly the same when we got into the common room, trying to devour a Mars bar, a packet of prawn cocktail crisps and a cold slab of pizza all at the same time.

"I spoke to Judy for a few minutes." Zoe eyed me warily, gauging my mood. I turned to my best friend, whose hair was stuck up like a hedgehog and whose mouth was bulging like a hamster's. I knew her well enough to know it wasn't good news.

86

"Claire has been in touch with her sister in Melbourne." Zoe drew in a deep bolstering breath. "Sid Shackleton is putting the money up for her to fly out here. Apparently she's got some evidence that should prove once and for all who Barney belongs to."

Tact had never been one of Zoe's strong points. The words battered against my eardrums refusing to take form. It was not what I wanted to hear. I felt as if all the drawbridges were clanking shut and there was nowhere left to run.

"Alex, are you all right?" Zoe nudged my shoulder. "You've gone as white as a sheet."

Mrs Brayfield's meeting to organize Eric's fiftieth birthday was scheduled for that evening at seven o'clock. There was a message on the answering machine for me to contact her, but all I could do was sit with my hands clamped together in my lap staring at a blow-up colour poster of Barney above the fridge and listening to the comings and goings of livery owners as all the horses were fed and tucked up for the night with fat hay nets and thick straw beds.

Zoe had gone home with the strict instructions that her dad would pick me up at six thirty. It was now twenty past five. I scratched the dirt out of my fingernails, starting with my left thumb and methodically drawing perfect half moons.

Then I picked up the mobile phone and hammered in six digits.

"Eric, it's Alex. I need to see you. I think I'm going out of my mind."

A cold breeze brushed my face and gently lifted my hair as I stood outside Eric's back door, tapping at the old-fashioned knocker and listening to Daisy's usual frenzy of barking.

I could hear Eric grumbling and flicking back the bolts, struggling with the bottom one, which desperately needed some oil. Then the warm cosy light flooded through the open door and I fell in, feeling the first racking sobs escape from my chest.

"The kettle's on, teabag's in the mug," muttered Eric. "I think you'd better go and sit down."

Daisy padded after me and lolloped into her favourite chair, slobbering over the arm in the hope of getting a titbit.

"Now what's the matter with you?" Eric thumped down a mug of steaming tea and was his usual non-sympathetic self.

"It's ... it's ..." I felt my face crumple and tears erupt like red-hot geysers into my eyes. Once they'd taken hold there was no stopping the volcano of emotion which I'd bottled up since that first visit from Sid Shackleton when I was stupid enough to think I'd been chosen for a national team.

Eric wheeled into the downstairs loo and came back with a full pink toilet roll which he thrust under my nose. "You've got three minutes of blubbering and then I want you to dry your face and tell me what all this is about."

I sniffed so loud Daisy came running across, hurling herself into my arms, and staring into my eyes with heartfelt concern. She pressed her damp nose into my hands and I gave her the biggest hug I could under the circumstances.

"Five, four, three . . ." Eric counted me down but all his mock-stern face did was make me cry harder.

"For heaven's sake, Alex, you'll make yourself ill at this rate. Now what on earth's happened?"

I told him about Claire's sister in Melbourne and how hopeless everything was and how I was at the end of my tether. By that time half the toilet roll was lying in wet shreds round my feet and Daisy was gnawing into the other half thinking it was some kind of soft bone.

"I can't go on," I finished, giving a deep, heart-trembling sigh and twisting a piece of toilet paper round my middle finger.

"So what are you going to do? Roll over and die?" Eric spat out the words with real hardness. "Fat lot of good that's going to do Barney."

"Why do you always have to be so tough?"

I screeched, angry at him now that he wasn't saying the right things.

"Because if I sympathize you're going to give up altogether and you're made of stronger stuff than that. You're a fighter, Alex, and I'm not going to let you crumple in a heap when the going starts to get tough."

"Tough?" I threw back at him. "It's a living nightmare."

"Now you listen to me." Eric waggled a finger at me as I tried to focus through a glaze of tears. "You've got backbone, girl, that's what sets you apart from everyone else. You never give up, you dig your heels in and you see things through."

"I used to," I sniffled, deflated.

"You still can, you've got to find that spark again. It's in there, in your heart. And while you've got that you can see this through to the end."

I stood up and walked shakily to the window where Eric had his collection of china Basset hounds and stared out at the army of molehills invading the soft mossy lawn.

"Alex?" Eric's voice was questioning, alert.

And as I turned round to face him, streams of tears drying on my cheeks, I made a momentous decision. And it was a decision that was going to change all our lives for ever.

CHAPTER NINE

I told my parents I was staying the night with
Zoe. They didn't suspect a thing.

I came back from Eric's and huddled in
Barney's stable under his blanket and waited until
everybody had left the yard. At the time I didn't
think that Zoe would wonder why I wasn't at
Mrs Brayfield's meeting. It didn't enter my head.
I didn't think that Ash might ring later to see
how I was coping. I was driven by a burning urge
to carry out my newly formed plan. And it had
to be tonight.

Barney could sense the anticipation and
rustled round his stable, one minute sniffing my
hair, next minute gazing out over his door. I
couldn't help but think how horses relied on us
for everything. We'd stripped them of their inde-
pendence and it was our duty to see they were
properly cared for.

A huge marble moon pushed plumply into
the darkened sky as I crouched in torchlight to
write a letter to my parents. How do you put into
words that you love them more than anyone in

the world but what you were about to do was necessary, it was the only way.

Darling Ash. How did I tell him that I'd probably never see him again? I pinched myself for being melodramatic and crept outside to say my goodbyes.

Lace, Zoe's grey pony, was standing quietly sleeping at the back of her stable. It seemed a lifetime ago since Zoe and I had started lessons with Eric, and Lace had been so good at the dressage, far better than Barney.

The Hawk. He'd sweetened up in the last six months and no longer put his ears back and pulled ugly faces. Camilla never appreciated how talented he really was.

Donavon. The gorgeous big chestnut Ash had all his hopes pinned on. Donavon never put a foot wrong.

Dolly was in the next stable. The young talented hopeful Eric was convinced would take Ash to the Olympics. She snuffled my hand and trembled as if she could sense my sadness.

George whickered noisily, determined not to be left out. I searched in my jacket pocket for some horse nuts which he gladly hoovered up. George with his big bay Roman nose and clumsy soup-plate feet. Would he ever take his jumping as seriously as he did his food? There was a champion locked inside that huge 16.3 body, it was just a matter of finding the right key.

Aching with emotion, I shook off a bout of fresh tears and headed back to Barney. I didn't have much time. I'd collected bits of old sacking and baling string from the barn earlier and now began the complicated process of tying them round Barney's hoofs to muffle the sound. It always looked so simple in films. Barney wasn't particularly helpful, trying to rip his front ones off with his teeth. An owl hooted outside and there was a mad flapping of wings. George stomped round his stable, neighing across the yard to Barney, his old pal. He was making enough noise to wake the dead.

I'd got a rucksack full of food from the common room and Ash's saddle bags stashed with things I thought we might need. My plan was to make my way to Blake Kildaire, who was a famous showjumping friend I'd met a few months before. He would take us in and maybe use his influence to put everything right. I remembered him telling me how he had kidnapped his star horse Colorado from a stuck-up girl called Louella and kept him at the horse and pony sanctuary, Hollywell Stables. If I could just get Barney there, they'd know what to do. They were experts.

The door creaked open as I led Barney out into the darkness. I knew I should have asked Ash or Eric for help but they were adamant about following the solicitor's advice. And so was Sir Charles. Barney nudged me in the back and that was the deciding factor. I truly couldn't bear for him to be taken away from me.

The grass was soft underfoot as we turned down the drive, spotlighted by the moon but hugging the post and rail fence and slipping away out of sight. We'd ride a good ten miles or so and then ring Hollywell Stables and get Blake to come and pick us up.

Barney started striding forward, his ears flapping back and forth, straining to hear some far-off noise. The Burgess drive was a long tarmac lane cutting through the parkland, about a quarter of a mile long with big iron gates at the bottom. Eric's cottage was tucked away behind the wood and there were no houses in sight. I closed my fingers round the phone number in my pocket and then pushed on.

It was only as we neared the bottom of the drive that I saw the figure running flat out towards us. A person was haring up the drive, obviously distraught, soft running shoes padding along the hard ground in rhythm. I could hear a rasping breathing.

There was nowhere to turn, nowhere to run. Any second now and he or she would see me.

We didn't stand a chance. We were going to get caught.

Claire Robinson lifted up her head and stared straight at me.

I'd never seen anybody look so pale and distraught. A huge black eye covered most of one side of her face. Her jeans and jacket were splattered with mud.

"What the hell do you want?" I was sizzling with white-hot anger. It was obvious she had some unhinged plan to steal Barney. Why else would she be running up our drive in the middle of the night? I loathed her. At that moment I wouldn't have thrown water on her if she'd been on fire.

Barney snatched at his bit and yanked me forward, thrusting his nose into her chest, tense with concern. Claire staggered back, leaning on the fence for support, looking on the verge of passing out. "It's all right," she gasped. "It's not what you think, I've come to talk – to . . . to tell the truth."

The old-fashioned kettle sat on the Aga whistling for attention, but I was too gobsmacked to pay any attention. I'd got into Ash's house by using the key kept under the begonia plant in the porch. His jeep was gone and there was a frantic message on the answering machine from Zoe to say that I'd disappeared and could he come over. His parents were still abroad and there was no one else in the house. It was the first place I could think of to take Claire. By this time she was hysterical and all I kept hearing were snatches of information all jumbled up and back to front.

I gave her some tea and waited for her to calm down. Ten minutes later her cheeks were flushing vivid pink and she started to make some sense. I dug in the freezer compartment of the fridge and gave her a mini bag of frozen peas to hold on her left eye which was swelling up like a golf ball. Barney was back in his stable tucking into his hay net, all plans abandoned in the light of Claire's confession. It hadn't really sunk in yet; I felt numb.

"So you see I always really loved him, even though he wasn't mine."

I took a slug of tea and collapsed in a chair, wanting to sob my heart out. This girl had sent me to hell and back and now she was saying it was all a pack of lies.

Claire Robinson had known Barney three years ago when he had belonged to gypsies and was named Dino. The gypsies had set up a camp on the local common and it quickly became apparent that they couldn't do a thing with Dino. He was a real renegade and kept escaping and going walkabout. Nobody could ride him and his owner, someone called Jed, was all for selling him for meat.

Then Claire came along and within minutes she'd befriended the horse; he would follow her round like a dog. Then she started riding him bareback and fixing up some jumps out of old mattresses and tyres, and it quickly became apparent that Dino had talent.

For nearly a year Claire looked after Dino as if he were her own. She would often ride him round her estate and even tie him up in her garden. Then she had to go away for a weekend to her granny's funeral and when she came back Dino had disappeared. Jed said he'd been stolen and Claire immediately reported it to the police and started knocking on doors and putting notices up in local shops.

Nothing. The gypsies moved on, disappearing one night in a moonlight flit. It was months afterwards that someone at the local riding school tipped Claire off that Dino had been sold at a horse auction. Nobody knew where he had gone. Claire became ill and thin and was literally pining away for the best part of a year. Then she managed to come out of it and Sid Shackleton offered her a job as general skivvy after she'd managed to stay on one of his most difficult horses. She'd completely put Dino out of her mind, finding it too painful to talk about.

Then one night she picked up the local paper to look at the Horses and Ponies column and there on the front page was Dino's picture screaming out at her, and a story of how he was destined to be a top eventer.

She'd confided in Shackleton and asked if he might take her to see Dino. Shackleton had cooked up the idea of pretending Dino was hers and everything seemed to fit. She had all his registration papers stashed away in her flat; she'd kept them as a memento. She had taken them out of Jed's caravan one day, not knowing how important they were to become. Shackleton promised that he would provide the finances for a lawyer if it had to go to court. In return she could have the ride on Dino and look after him as her own.

It was only last night that she'd found out the real truth, that Shackleton had already found a buyer for Dino in Germany and they were talking about a huge amount of money. Graham was going to get five hundred pounds cash for encouraging Claire to go through with it. She had been used left, right and centre and now all she could do was try to put things right.

"I've been a stupid fool." She smothered her face in her hands. "I was so hell-bent on getting Dino back I never stopped to think how you must be feeling. I know you must hate me but I thought I could give him a better home."

"I love him," I said simply, forcing my mouth not to tremble.

"I know." She gave a small laugh etched with sadness. "I do too."

I asked her about her eye.

"It was Graham. The thought of losing his five hundred pounds was too much. He'd had too much to drink and thought he could knock some sense into me." Instinctively she touched the bruise and winced. "Another of my great mistakes."

"I'm sorry," I said, and truly meant it. I abhorred violence and even though Ash was up on an assault charge I knew that he was innocent. "It was really brave of you, I mean to come here, to run away from Graham and tell the truth, but I can't forgive you, not yet, not for a while anyway."

Claire scuffled in her pocket and pulled out a bundle of papers which she pushed across the table. Barney's registration papers and a height certificate. "I think these belong to you. If you don't mind, I'd like to keep the photos."

CHAPTER TEN

Ash stormed into the kitchen. Claire tactfully went outside for some air.

"How could you have been so stupid?" Ash was beside himself with anger. "I thought I'd managed to make you see sense, but you try and run away? Alex, what were you thinking of?"

"Well, all right, there's no need to go on," I cringed.

"What hare-brained scheme are you going to come up with next, that's what I want to know." Ash looked impossibly tired. There were giant black smudges under his eyes and his shoulders sagged. "You're headstrong and stubborn and impulsive."

"I know." Suddenly I started to laugh and cry at the same time. I wanted to dance round the kitchen. It felt like the end of the war. "It's all over," I shrieked. "Barney's mine for ever and I've got the papers to prove it!"

Ash went to call off the search and round everyone up. He came back, screeching the jeep tyres on the gravel outside, with Zoe and Mrs

Brayfield and Sir Charles following behind in a BMW. They rushed in, Mrs Brayfield giving a yelp when she saw me and exclaiming that they all thought I'd done a runner.

"Well, I . . . the thing is . . ."

Then their eyes fell on Claire, sitting hunched and guilt-stricken at the table, her blackened eye, half hidden in shadow, and the bag of frozen peas melting and dripping into her lap.

"I think I've got a lot of explaining to do." Claire scraped back her chair and stood up. For a split second I almost felt sorry for her. It was like facing the Grand Jury.

Claire told us all about Sid Shackleton and his various ways of extracting money from innocent people. She also said that he had worked out that Zoe was from the Burgess yard and her intentions were more than just improving her dressage – she was desperately trying to catch him out. A little research by ringing Zoe's school proved that she was my best friend.

Claire had seen and heard Shackleton go berserk when Jesse told him that he'd followed Zoe home and that their suspicions were correct.

"The kid knows nothing, she was just snooping." Jesse had tried to pacify him.

All the time Claire was crouched in the hayloft above, spying through a crack in the floorboards and trembling with the fear of being caught.

Shackleton's ringing voice could have cut through steel. "You'd better keep a close eye on that Judy bird, she could be from the same camp."

Jesse moved back a step so that Claire could see the thinning bald patch in his soft brown hair. Jesse had developed a soft spot for Judy and tried to cover for her. He insisted she was a first-class groom and hated the Burgess family.

"All the same, if she finds out too much . . ."

"Don't worry." Jesse tried to control a hint of irritation. "She's OK, trust me. She knows nothing."

Claire's stomach had gone on to spin-dry. The hay seeds were building up in her nose and felt like a hundred ants crawling inside her nostrils. Shackleton paced up and down, his great stomach sticking out in front of him. "Ring up the Greens," he suddenly barked. "Tell them to pick up Red Cloud at nine o'clock in the morning. We're taking no risks."

Jesse hovered towards the door. "And keep an eye on Claire – we've got to have that yellow nag soon or else the Germans will lose interest. I want to clean up on this deal. We're talking megabucks. We'll deal with the girl once we've sold the horse. She shouldn't be too hard to pay off."

Shackleton barged out of the tack room after

Jesse, totally unaware that they'd been overheard. Claire waited long minutes and then sat back on her heels, wrapping her arms round her rigid body and gently rocking back and forth. For the first time in her short life, Claire Robinson felt as if she could commit murder . . .

"So you see if somebody doesn't stop him he'll just go on and on. He's a bully and a cheat and he uses his position in the horse world as the perfect cover. The man's a toad."

"The police are finally taking it seriously." Sir Charles crashed into a chair in the kitchen, chucking his sheepskin bomber jacket over towards the radiator, and missing so it landed on Daisy. "We're meeting them there tomorrow morning."

The old-fashioned clock in the kitchen made everybody's nerves twang as it proudly pealed the twelve chimes of midnight.

"There's absolutely no way we can contact Judy before then?" Sir Charles was blaming himself for Judy's potential danger.

"She's a tough girl." Ash tried to reassure him. "She can look after herself."

But looking after headstrong, unpredictable horses wasn't the same as being faced with Sid Shackleton, Graham, and Jesse.

Ash shot me a worry-tinged look. Judy was

in the enemy camp and she had no idea what was going on.

The olive-green Land Rover Discovery surged left under the sign Wideacre Stud, which was Sid Shackleton's establishment. A matching green trailer glided behind, both partitions empty, ready to pick up Red Cloud. I could imagine their excitement – like everyone when they are buying their first horse.

A police car was parked in front of us, hidden down a side road biding their time. It was five minutes past nine. We had to hang on, wait until the dodgy deal was done. A gaggle of colts and a filly came hurtling up pushing inquisitive noses into a thorn hedge. All we needed now was a groom to come and spring us and the whole plan would be shot to pieces.

Ash squeezed my hand. We could practically hear each other's heart beating.

Sir Charles snatched at the ignition, turning the key frantically. "Come on, we're off!"

The police car lurched ahead in front of us. The next few minutes were a blur. All I remember is the quivering face of Sid Shackleton twitching in speechless horror.

"Sir, I'm arresting you under suspicion of fraud. You have the right to remain silent . . ."

Shackleton looked as if he were going to

explode. "You're doing what? Get your hands off me – this is ridiculous."

His mean eyes suddenly fixed on mine, shooting out a flood of venom. "What's that girl been telling you? It's her you should be arresting – she's the one harbouring a stolen pony."

The police officer carried on reading him his rights.

"This is outrageous," he barked. "I'm on my way to a meeting for the Horse of the Year show. Have you any idea just who you're dealing with?"

"A conman." Sir Charles stepped out of the back of his tinted-window Mercedes with Claire at his side. "This is the end of the line, Shackleton. I suggest you give these good people their money back – you've already done enough damage."

Mr and Mrs Green gawped in shock, glancing from the trailer to Shackleton to the police officer in confusion. Mrs Green suddenly latched on to Sir Charles.

"Mrs Green, we have every reason to believe that the horse in your trailer is not the one you originally agreed to buy."

"Liar!" Shackleton lunged forward, fighting to get free.

"This is a racket that Mr Shackleton has been up to for some time."

"You self-righteous, interfering fool . . ."

"Mr Shackleton, would you please restrain

yourself." The police officer was going redder in the face.

Mrs Green promptly burst into tears.

"Where's Judy?" Ash lunged forward, towering over Shackleton, at his most threatening. There was no sign of any staff anywhere.

Shackleton's eyes flickered across to the stables on the left. Ash was there in seconds, flinging back the doors, startling the horses who all looked so hauntingly alike.

"Come on, Shackleton, where is she?" Ash was coming to the end of the line. "Judy?" His voice was more of a rasp.

The last door whined back on its hinges and Graham leapt out, pushing Ash full on the chest.

"Get him!" Sir Charles hurled himself forward.

"Graham, stop it, you can't escape!" Claire was screeching at the top of her voice, but Graham shot down the side of the stables and hurdled a wheelbarrow. Ash was after him.

The horse who was in the last stable ran through the open door heading straight for the barn on the other side of the yard. All we could hear were Graham's screams and the horse's scrabbling hoofs.

"It was nothing to do with me!" Graham bleated as Ash threw his weight on him and they both keeled over.

Shackleton's face crumpled as Graham babbled on in a desperate bid to offload the blame. All he succeeded in doing was confessing to everything and proving Shackleton's guilt.

Nobody else heard the plaintive scream for help coming from a closed door marked FEED ROOM which the loose horse was pacing up and down outside. I only heard because I'd moved across to try and catch him and I was quite a distance away from the others.

"Judy!"

I heard something crash to the ground.

"Judy!"

The feed room door was bolted top and bottom but not locked. I pulled back both bolts and flung the door open and there was Judy, her wrists and ankles bound with baling string and a strip of tape across her mouth which she'd managed to half rub off.

I quickly fumbled to undo the tape. "Have you caught them?" she yelled, as soon as I'd freed her mouth.

"They're in the police car." Ash bent down, pulling at the taut knots at her wrists. "Oh Judy, what have they done to you?"

"Never mind me," she said.

The bay horse stuck its nose round the doorway, its velvety brown eyes gleaming at Judy.

"Tell the Greens, that's their horse! I've been looking after him for the past ten days!"

Sid Shackleton, Graham, and the head groom Jesse would probably all be facing a stint in prison or an extremely hefty fine. It would take months to uncover the true extent of Shackleton's crimes but according to Sir Charles it easily ran into hundreds of thousands of pounds worth of fraud.

The Greens were going to be the lucky owners of the bay horse nicknamed Sid who was probably the only decent dressage horse in Shackleton's stable. Judy explained how she'd been so bored at the stables just doing mucking out and no riding that she'd been practising a new training method she'd seen on television, based on behavioural patterns. It worked instantly and after just a day he was following her around like a pet dog.

"I think he sees me as a big sister," she laughed, setting herself up easily for Ash to joke that she'd always resembled a horse.

Judy had promised Mrs Green that she'd go and stay with them in Dorset and help her with Sid and hopefully fast-forward the bonding process.

We all agreed to go out for a meal that night as a celebration and what was originally meant as a meal for five turned into a heaving great party of twelve which meant three tables had to be pushed together and those crammed at the back had to climb under their table to go to the toilet. It was bedlam.

Eric mysteriously refused to come but sent a gorgeous congratulations card with a one-day event schedule tucked inside. I mentally programmed myself to take Barney some cake home in a doggy bag.

When the meal was over we discussed Eric's birthday surprise. Cam whipped out a notepad from her bag and reeled off a list of plans and things to do.

"Are you sure he's going to like it? I mean, it's a bit unconventional," said Toukie.

"I suppose you'd want a strippergram and a personal appearance from the Chippendales," Cam snorted, giving Toukie a withering look.

Mrs Brayfield was just about to venture under the table to the loos when Sir Charles' mobile phone vibrated into life.

"Sssssh!" Ash tried to lower the noise by a hundred decibels.

Sir Charles hovered by the window to get a better reception.

"Well, Eric, you sly old dog, you've really taken the biscuit this time."

Ash looked at me as my head sprang upright on red alert. "What's going on?" he mouthed.

I shrugged my shoulders.

"That was Eric." Sir Charles clicked off the phone and returned to the table.

"Talk of the devil." Jasper filled up his glass and forgot about everybody else's. "What did he want? Were his ears burning?"

"It sounds as if he's been ringing every important horsy person in the country." Sir Charles sat down with an air of gravity. "That's one hell of an uncle you've got there, Ash." Sir Charles asked everybody to raise their glasses even though half of them were empty.

"A toast." He held up his glass. "To Eric's tenacity and Ash's future." A clump of rust-red hair fell forward over his brow. "The suspension's been lifted!"

CHAPTER ELEVEN

"I should never have let you talk me into this."
Ash was sitting on an upturned bucket by the side
of the horsebox suffering from a serious bout of
nerves.

It was the Darleybrook three-day event, a
new course owned by the Hollywood actress
Elissa Donahue who was throwing a fortune into
eventing and made it quite clear she wanted the
star part in a remake of International Velvet. It
was rumoured she had taken up riding after dating
the gorgeous Ben McCarthy and then becoming
close friends of the Webb-Lloyds. She was quoted
as saying, "If Oliver Skeete can ride and stay on,
then so can I, and by the way, he can take me out
to dinner to discuss related distances any night of
the week." The *Mirror* had made a big piece of it
and since then she'd become the darling of
Horse and Hound and a model for George Golder
jodhpurs and horsewear.

The only trouble with Darleybrook Castle
was that it was stuck in the middle of nowhere
on the edge of a moorland in Cumbria with

nothing but heather and acres of billowing black sky.

The practice ring was a churning mass of mud.

George huddled in his portable wooden stable rolling his eyes at the roof as if it was going to crash in on his head. Judy had fixed up two jumbo hay nets the night before which had been devoured and he'd had a bucket of corn this morning. Keeping George's waistline in trim was a near impossible juggling act. If he thought he was being deprived of food he simply refused to work.

Ash covered his head with a show programme as the first heavy blobs of rain started to descend.

"I must be out of my mind," he groaned, clutching at his stomach and then making a mad dash for the nearest portaloo. "I'll never be able to hold him at this rate."

Despite rubber reins and special gloves with a revolutionary sticky palm, anchoring George in a deluge of rain, hurtling over moorland at a flat-out gallop, sounded like a recipe for disaster.

Eric had insisted on trying a new Citation bridle which Ginny Leng had used on Murphy Himself and Eric promised would have an effect. When we first fitted the contraption George went in for some equine dramatics, spinning round on his heels and putting in a volley of hefty bucks until he realized he was fighting a losing battle. The proof of the pudding would be when he came down the terrifying Darleybrook Drop in collected canter.

Nicknamed the Death Drop, we'd stood and examined fence nine with disbelief and reeling horror. Nobody was sure if it was even jumpable. If it kept raining the take-off would be treacherous and a horse out of control would be sure to somersault. Three people had officially complained and five pulled out. William Fox-Pitt said it was the kind of fence you'd expect on an Olympic track. Ash was convinced that Eric was out of his mind and George was way out of his class.

Eric had arrived just as George had finished his dressage test. For once he had his brain in gear and did a reliable test to finish in equal third.

Then we set off to walk the cross-country in sou'westers and oil-proof trousers fighting against torrential sweeps of rain and freezing temperatures more suitable for November. Judy was convinced she'd spotted Mel Gibson in dark glasses escorting Elissa Donahue to the Trout Hatchery but it was too muggy to tell for sure.

Eric had driven as near as he could to the Darleybrook Drop and then Ash had pushed him through the squelchy mud to the edge of the sheer drop, which the horse wouldn't see until the very

115

last minute. Even worse there was a sequence of bounces running downhill which was part of the complex and demanded ultra-skill as a rider. The horse's mind would still be on the bounces and the drop would take it completely by surprise.

Ash stared glumly down the drop which had sand layered down at the take-off. "He'll never do it," he said in a flat voice. "He's not light enough on his feet. It's like asking Robbie Coltrane to do Riverdance."

"Oh, don't be so wet," Eric snapped at him, ignoring the drops of rain ricocheting off everybody's noses. "It's up to you to hold him together."

"I agree," Judy chipped in, faintly critical. "George has hidden depths, you've got to have faith in him."

Two women strutted past us in jodhpurs so tight they made their thighs look like suet puddings. "I don't know what all the fuss is about," one of them chirruped in an artificially cultured voice. "Just sit tight and kick on!"

Eric's face wrinkled in disdain and then he started telling us how it should really be jumped.

"Don't come in too fast." His eyes sparkled. "Steady a little in front of the fence, make sure he's off his forehand, then keep coming forward in a steady rhythm."

I'd read endlessly about how if you went too fast over a drop fence you pitched more weight onto the horse's forehand and he was more likely to buckle on landing or lose his balance. Coming in a little on the deep side of the take-off point helps the horse to see where he is going to land.

"Don't jump at an angle." Eric became so passionate his cheeks turned red. "You've got to come in dead straight. If he does twist, at least you'll stay together."

Ash's face had gone distinctly yellow and he shot me a very unsteady smile.

"Don't forget to slip the reins," said Eric. Zoe hung her head, no doubt remembering falling off Lace because her hands had been so welded to the reins.

"Got it," Ash grumbled, fidgeting with his feet. "Will you organize the ambulance or shall I?"

Eric had been the one to force Ash into entering George for Darleybrook, even though all the big names were turning out, because it was a Badminton qualifier.

The Horse Trials officials had been so impressed by Eric's determination to end Ash's suspension that they hadn't objected to George's late entry. They wanted as little publicity about Sid Shackleton as possible but even so it had taken a phone call from Eric to the American who'd originally taken the photographs to seal their goodwill. There was a whole sequence of pictures showing that Ash was innocent. The American had suddenly swapped sides when he heard about Shackleton's arrest and admitted to being paid off.

Our original plan for Eric's surprise birthday party had had to be cancelled because it clashed with Darleybrook. What on earth could we do in the middle of Cumbria, sitting in a deluge, in a horsebox with no heating and only tinned food and chocolate biscuits. All the local hotels were booked chock-a-block and the nearest restaurant was forty miles away. Elissa hardly ever stayed at the castle and was flying back to London that night by helicopter.

The last thing on Ash's mind was partying. It was the morning of the cross-country and the only person who had taken the direct route at the Death Drop had landed flat on their face. The alternative added on an extra minute. The international names would surely all go straight on and if Ash was to stand any chance of a place he'd have to join them.

George was like a queen bee surrounded by workers, Judy frantically taping up his tail, Zoe screwing in studs and Eric barking instructions and checking the bandages and boots were fitted exactly right.

Ash had to be out on roads and tracks precisely five minutes later. He was pacing up and down muttering that his spurs were the wrong pair and he was going to make a complete fool of himself.

"Ash Burgess, pull yourself together and get on this horse and prove yourself." Eric wheeled up behind him, making us both jump out of our skins.

"You can do it." I added my encouragement, grabbing hold of Ash's hand and squeezing it to death. "You've just got to believe in George."

"Three, two, one . . . *Go!*" George's swinging bay bottom disappeared down the road on Phase A of roads and tracks. All we could do now was wait. And pray.

"Remember to anchor him, don't let him get his head down. And keep your legs on, right till the very last stride."

George spun round in circles as Eric blasted Ash with last-minute instructions. We were in the ten-minute halt box at the start of the cross-country. Andrew Michaelson was out on the course scorching his way towards the Darleybrook Drop. George looked fantastic, his glossy lustrous coat covering hard-packed muscle, his big open eyes alert and honest. Ash shot me a stomach-liquidizing smile and then they were off, George blasting up to the first fence at his usual reckless pelt.

119

"Settle down, settle down." Eric grabbed the binoculars; Judy, Zoe and I scoured round for the nearest TV monitor.

George was really flying.

"If that 'oss was grey, he'd be called Desert Orchid," someone leaning on a walking stick shouted as George leapt a fence two strides out and then let out a buck of pure exhilarated joy.

Ash kept ultra cool, with a steady rein contact. The Darleybrook Drop was coming up next and George was bounding on, fighting for his head.

Ash leaned back and closed his fingers. George kept on coming. He looked as if he was going to slide straight into the first of the bounces. Ash fought desperately to get him on the right stride. Up until now the Citation bridle had been working miracles.

"Hold him, Ash!"

George stood back to take off, than changed his mind and visibly hesitated, his legs flailing. With amazing calm, Ash gathered up the reins, clamped on his legs, and yelled, "Get over!"

George put in a superhorse effort. Ash held tight and then yanked on the brakes to set himself up for the drop. George responded and went into a neat bouncy canter.

"Way to go, Ash!" Zoe was going slightly bonkers with excitement.

George showed himself a champion and a braveheart as he leapt into space at Ash's request. It was an incredible sight, horse and rider in perfect harmony, at full stretch, trusting each other. And that was what good riding was all about. Faith in each other.

"Yes!"

George touched down without pecking and surged on for the next fence.

"Brilliant!" Eric punched the air. Zoe flung her arms round my neck and nearly blocked off my windpipe. The commentator was going mad. I felt sick with relief that my boyfriend was still in one piece.

"He's up on the time!" The commentator was frantically checking against other competitors. George was really opening out now in a thunderous gallop between fences, Ash laid low over his withers.

"That's a Badminton horse." A thin knowing smile filtered across the face of the man next to me.

Eric smirked and winked at me. George was out there proving himself a champion. He was no longer in Donavon's shadow, clumsy footed and a bit goofy. He'd matured into a jumping machine of amazing power. Ash must feel as if he was on board a rocket.

He flew over the last fence and bounded up

121

to the finish line looking as if he'd only just started.

Ash jumped off and I hurtled across, throwing my arms round both of them, mud and sweat smearing down my neck and then turning round to realize the TV cameras were right on top of us and zooming in for a close-up.

Ash started singing George's praises and thanking everybody involved. He mentioned Eric and then his girlfriend who was a permanent tower of strength. That was me. It was the first time he'd mentioned to the media that he had a girlfriend and I blushed and quickly buried my head in George's neck.

George gave me an affectionate nudge in the ribs.

"Come on, boy, I think we've had enough excitement for one day." Judy ran forward with a sweat rug and we led our hero off to the stables while Ash weighed in and fought off a sea of fans.

Zoe raced up as Judy and I tied up George in his stable with a hay net and started the laborious job of removing all the leg grease.

Zoe was pink in the face and stuttering for the first time in her life. "George is way out in the lead." She was almost hysterical. "The first three leading riders are all out," she gasped. "Unless George bulldozes the showjumping he's the winner. He's got about six fences in hand."

I whooped in delight and then Ash came in looking impossibly tired but ecstatic. "It looks like that interfering uncle of mine was right again," he grinned.

And then he wrapped his arms round me and nearly squeezed the breath out of me.

Eric was as proud as punch of the birthday surprise we'd organized for him. At the last minute Cam's boyfriend Aaron had managed to persuade his dad to loan him a forty-ton truck and a driver which all the Pony Club members had decked out with drapes, tables, party streamers, posters, pictures of Eric as a young man and all his lifetime achievements, and the carriage clock they'd all chipped in to buy which we'd had specially engraved.

Aaron and Mrs Brayfield sat in the luxury cab as the truck trundled onto the showground by special permission and we celebrated Eric's fifteenth birthday with a champagne and fish and chip party in a truck on a Cumbrian moor. The atmosphere was fantastic and more than once I saw tears in Eric's eyes.

A total surprise to me was the arrival of Barney in Cam's mother's trailer. He had apparently been getting up to so much mischief at home that they thought it would be easier to bring him with them. Barney settled in with George for a good gossip and we all agreed that George was giving him a blow by blow account of the cross-country and Barney was listening like an old hand.

"Hip hip hooray!" We all sang Happy Birthday badly out of tune, refrained from giving Eric the bumps and instead sprung the main surprise which we'd been keeping undercover until this moment.

Sir Charles stood up, nearly knocking over the flimsy table, and called for everybody's attention. Eric had apparently been invited to a special parade at the Horse of the Year show for his outstanding contribution to the horse world. It was an honour and a privilege and Eric had to turn away for a few minutes to gather his composure.

If anyone truly deserved such an award it was Eric. He'd given his life, his health and his soul to horses. And in an emotional speech he said he'd do it all again if he had the choice. He was a privileged man and horses had enriched his life. Even if horses like Barney had stacked on the wrinkles and grey hairs of late!

Sir Charles raised his glass for a toast. And it was simply, "To Eric."

George did his showjumping round at 3.30 the following afternoon and performed an immaculate clear. The clapping and cheers were ear-popping as he rode out of the ring, and Barney was parading round in his best rug like Red Rum, no doubt taking the glory for giving George advice.

Ash and George had clinched the Darleybrook trophy and set themselves on an illustrious path to Badminton. Elissa Donahue presented the trophy, kissing Ash rather too passionately, and all the horse magazines and dailies were there to catch the moment.

Barney tugged me off to a pretty grey mare standing in the collecting ring and a huge smile broke out on my lips, and a familiar stinging in my eyes. Barney was mine, lock, stock and barrel for ever and ever. And I was so proud I could have burst with happiness.

GLOSSARY

anti-cast roller   A stable **roller** which prevents the horse from becoming **cast** in the stable or box.

Badminton   One of the world's greatest three-day events, staged each year at Badminton House, Gloucestershire.

to bank   When a horse lands on the middle part of an obstacle (e.g. a **table**), it is said to have banked it.

BHS points   British Horse Society method of categorizing a horse's experience and ability.

bit   The part of the bridle which fits in the mouth of the horse, and to which the reins are attached.

bounce   A type of jump consisting of two fences spaced so that as the horse lands from the first, it takes off for the next, with no strides in between.

bridle   The leather **tack** attached to the horse's head which helps the rider to control the horse.

Burghley Major three-day event.

cast When a horse is lying down against a wall in a stable or box and is unable to get up, it is said to be cast.

cavaletti Small wooden practice jump.

chef d'équipe The person who manages and sometimes captains a team at events.

coffin A challenging cross-country jump, consisting of a jump in, a bounce or stride to a ditch, and then a bounce or stride to another jump.

colic A sickness of the digestive system. Very dangerous for horses because they cannot be sick.

collected canter A slow pace with good energy.

crop A whip.

cross-country A gallop over rough ground, jumping solid natural fences. One of the three eventing disciplines. (The others are **dressage** and **showjumping**.)

dressage A discipline in which rider and horse perform a series of movements to show how balanced, controlled, etc. they are.

drop fence Cross-country fence where the ground on the take-off side is higher than that on the landing side.

dun Horse colour, generally yellow dun. (Also blue dun.)

feed room Store room for horse food.

forearm The part of the foreleg between elbow and knee.

girth The band which goes under the stomach of a horse to hold the **saddle** in place.

Grackle A type of noseband which stops the horse opening its mouth wide or crossing its jaw.

half pass A **dressage** movement.

hand A hand is 10 cm (4 in) – approximately the width of a man's hand. A horse's height is given in hands.

hard mouth A horse is said to have a hard mouth if it does not respond to the rider's commands through the **reins** and **bit**. It is caused by over-use of the reins and bit: the horse has got used to the pressure and thus ignores it.

head collar A headpiece without a **bit**, used for leading and tying-up.

Hitchcock gag A more efficient and strict version of the classic gag bridle, using two sets of pulleys.

horsebox A vehicle designed specifically for the transport of horses.

horse trailer A trailer holding one to three horses, designed to be towed by a separate vehicle.

jockey skull A type of riding hat, covered in brightly coloured silks or nylon.

jodhpurs Type of trousers/leggings worn when riding.

lead rope Used for leading a horse. (Also known as a "shank".)

livery Stables where horses are kept at the owners' expense.

loose box A stable or area, where horses can be kept.

manege Enclosure for schooling a horse.

manger Container holding food, often fixed to a stable wall.

martingale Used to regulate a horse's head carriage.

numnah Fabric pad shaped like a saddle and worn underneath one.

one-day event Equestrian competition completed over one day, featuring **dressage, showjumping** and **cross-country**.

one-paced Describes a horse which prefers to move at a certain pace, and is unwilling to speed up or increase its stride.

over-reach boots Used for preventing or protecting wounds caused when the hind legs strike the back of the forelegs, causing over-reaching.

Palomino A horse with a gold-coloured body and white mane or tail.

Pelham bit A bit with a curb chain and two **reins**, for use on horses that are hard to stop.

Pony Club International youth organization, founded to encourage young people to ride.

reins Straps used by the rider to make contact with a horse's mouth and control it.

roller Leather or webbing used to keep a rug or blanket in place. Like a belt or girth which goes over the withers and under the stomach.

rustic poles Unpainted jumping poles.

saddle Item of tack which the rider sits on. Gives security and comfort and assists in controlling the horse.

schoolmaster horse A horse or pony which has been well trained, making it ideal for inexperienced riders.

showjumping A course of coloured jumps that can be knocked down. Shows how careful and controlled horse and rider are.

snaffle bit The simplest type of **bit**.

spread Type of jump involving two uprights at increasing heights.

square halt Position where the horse stands still with each leg level, forming a rectangle.

steeplechasing A horse race with a set number of obstacles including a water jump. Originally a cross-country race from steeple to steeple.

stirrups Shaped metal pieces which hang from the saddle by leather straps and into which riders place their feet.

surcingle A belt or strap used to keep a day or night rug in position. Similar to a **roller,** but without padding.

table A type of jump built literally like a table, with a flat top surface.

tack Horse-related items.

tack room Where tack is stored.

take-off The point when a horse lifts its forelegs and springs up to jump.

ten-minute halt box Area for enforced rest period between roads and tracks and cross-country.

three-day event A combined training competition, held over three consecutive days. Includes **dressage, cross-country** and **showjumping**. Sometimes includes roads and tracks.

tiger trap A solid fence meeting in a point with a large ditch underneath. Large ones are called elephant traps.

trotting poles Wooden poles placed at intervals on the ground to improve a horse's pacing.

trout hatchery A water jump where the horse jumps in and out again.

upright A normal single showjumping fence.

Weymouth bit Like a **Pelham bit,** but more severe.

Samantha Alexander

RIDERS 7

Perfect Timing

"It was you, wasn't it? You did the robbery. You're wearing my sister's ring."

Dominic lunged forward, grabbing Tony Lucas by the shirt and crashing him back against the table.

"No!" I shrieked, panic tearing through me. "You'll kill him!"

Dominic Davidson is intelligent, sensitive and a gifted rider. But he's in trouble and only Alex can save him from a police arrest . . .

Samantha Alexander

RIDERS 8

Winning Streak

"Don't you see?" Blake's eyes flooded with fear. "Somebody's after Colorado. They want to put him out of action."

He pulled me round to the stables where somebody had been busy with a spray can: "PULL OUT OF MEADSTEAD – OR ELSE!"

Blake Kildaire is the heart-throb of the showjumping world, and the Sutton Valley Pony Club can't believe their luck when he comes to give them lessons. But there's a prankster in their midst with sinister motives . . .